LILY AND TAYLOR

LILY
AND
TAYLOR

ELISE MOSER

Groundwood Books
House of Anansi Press
Toronto Berkeley

Epigraph quote from "Castle Walk," in *Now You Care* by Di Brandt (Coach House Books, 2003). Used by permission.

Groundwood Books / House of Anansi Press
110 Spadina Avenue, Suite 801, Toronto, Ontario M5V 2K4
or c/o Publishers Group West
1700 Fourth Street, Berkeley, CA 94710

We acknowledge for their financial support of our publishing program the Canada Council for the Arts, the Government of Canada through the Canada Book Fund (CBF) and the Ontario Arts Council.

 Canada Council   Conseil des Arts    ONTARIO ARTS COUNCIL
for the Arts   du Canada   CONSEIL DES ARTS DE L'ONTARIO

Library and Archives Canada Cataloguing in Publication
Moser, Elise
Lily and Taylor / written by Elise Moser.
Issued also in electronic format.
ISBN 978-1-55498-334-6 (bound).—ISBN 978-1-55498-335-3 (pbk.)
I. Title.
PS8626.O8425L54 2013   jC813'.6   C2013-900394-0

Cover illustration by Vivienne Flesher
Design by Michael Solomon

Printed and bound in Canada

MIX
Paper from
responsible sources
FSC® C016245
FSC
www.fsc.org

Somewhere deep inside us
the centre holds.
— Di Brandt

One

THEY STUFFED HER BRAIN into her chest.

That was what surprised Taylor most. Not the smell. Not how matter-of-fact it was. Thinking back, she'd understood from the way the police arrived and walked — didn't run — across the grass that this stuff happened every day. There was something horrible about murder being ordinary, but it had made her feel calmer. Someone would know what to do. They had done it before.

Now there was this weird double-sidedness to everything. The gleaming tile-and-steel of the morgue was eerie, like the inside of a UFO or something. On the other hand, the tile in the washroom was the same dull pink as in school. The paper-towel dispenser stuck, also the same as in school. And the people doing the autopsy were completely ordinary, the technician's soft red hair held back in a simple black plastic clip. There was something creepy about that, too — like everything should be super serious here.

But then, Taylor reflected, taking a big drag off her cigarette, it was ordinary. At the morgue it was just another day. For herself, she wanted it to feel somehow final.

Taylor had been here before. She'd come for the identification. The woman police officer said Taylor wasn't allowed, but she saw the man officer hesitate, and something made her insist.

"I can do it," she said, her heart fluttering wildly in her chest.

"It's not good for you. It's too hard for kids," the man said. Taylor just stood there. After what had happened, seeing Tannis lying still and peaceful didn't sound too hard. Besides, she couldn't bear the thought of not seeing her sister one last time.

"I could get in trouble," the officer said gently. They didn't talk any more about it. But when a guy in a suit arrived and walked through, the man officer looked away, and Taylor slipped into the elevator behind the guy.

She felt reassured seeing the body, cold and clean and white and scraped and final, lying there on the stainless-steel tray, the giant dark bruise blooming on Tannis's forehead. She almost wished she could bring Mason. She thought he would feel better if he could picture Tannis dead, and not just vaguely disappeared. Taylor didn't want him to wonder in his little mind if his mother was out there somewhere, having a life without him.

The last time they'd seen Tannis, she was flying in a whirl of blood and there had been so much screaming they couldn't pay attention to anything except getting out of the way and staying out of it while Bracken killed Tannis every way he could think of. Smashing into her with his truck, getting out and yelling at her as she tried to stand up, grabbing the ax handle at the side of the garage and hitting her with it, pounding her with his big hands. So much rage came off his red face in waves, it seemed like it was slamming into Tannis, too.

They'd seen stuff like that before, though, and every other time Tannis had been alive after all.

Sometimes she was just wiping a bloody nose, her puffed lips twisting — gently, so it wouldn't hurt so much. Other times she only came to in a hospital bed, wrapped in plaster like a school art project, her eyes little galaxies of bloody veins and her fingers poking out the ends of her casts, flexing gingerly in the movement that even Mason knew meant she wanted a cigarette.

In contrast, the autopsy was deeply calm. The technicians sliced into Tannis with their shiny scalpels as if she were a strange white fruit. They sawed at her bones as if she were a fallen tree, snipped with their long silvery scissors the way Gram cut the thread one time when she hemmed Taylor's jeans. They weighed Tannis's heart and brain as if they were at a butcher counter.

When everything was drained, weighed and measured, the technician held Tannis open like a duffel bag and repacked the empty chest cavity with her heart, liver, kidneys and brain, laying the fat gray-yellow blob inside with the red organs.

Then they sewed Tannis up with big black stitches.

|||||

In the hotel, Gram was watching her program and smoking in that chicken-peck way she had, dipping the end of the cigarette between her lips and plucking it out again just as fast.

Taylor found Mason in the bathroom, face red and dirty, striped cotton T-shirt dirty, too. He was sitting in the bathtub, his shoes pressed up against the sides of the tub at a funny angle. He hummed as he constructed something out of the big, brightly colored pop-together plastic blocks that littered the stained white enamel, a thin dribble of saliva creeping down his chin as he concentrated.

He didn't look up when Taylor opened the door, but something broke in his attention. Taylor knew he could see her out of the corners of his eyes. He had perfected this skill living with Bracken for half of his short life. It was always best to know where Bracken was and what kind of mood he was in, although not always best to let him see you seeing.

Taylor reached over and laid a light hand on Mason's sandy head, and his gaze flicked upward. She knew he was glad to see her.

She pulled the bathroom door almost closed again and flopped down in the chair next to the sofa where Gram was sitting. Gram waited until a commercial and then looked up.

"Hungry?" she asked, her voice flat. It was surprisingly girlish but with an edge of gravel from a lifetime of smoking. On the side table was a yellow cardboard box surrounded by dirty paper plates and crumpled paper napkins.

Taylor leaned over the arm of the chair and lifted the box lid. Inside was a cold fried chicken breast, the breading split across the middle where it had been cut with a knife, the fibers of whitish meat visible inside.

She suddenly felt dizzy. She levered herself up on one

hip across the arm of the chair to push the box as close to the wall as she could. Then she quickly scrabbled her last smoke out of the box and lit it, inhaling as if it was all the food she needed.

Gram had already swiveled her eyes back to the television, although it was still running commercials.

"See what you wanted to see?" Gram asked, her voice still mostly empty.

Taylor didn't answer. The smoke from her cigarette curled over her fingers.

"You be ready to go home tomorrow?" Gram asked, still without looking over. "I gotta get back to Douglas. I only left him three dinners in the freezer."

Taylor heaved a sigh. The program played out its last segment and then Gram raised the remote and clicked it off. She reached to the edge of the nearest bed and rummaged in her purse, pulling out a ten and a twenty.

"Here, honey. I know you're out of cigarettes, and you can get some hot food in you, too. You could use that." Gram came near and used the side of the hand holding the money to push Taylor's hair off her forehead.

Taylor felt the prickling behind her eyes. A dam's worth of water was threatening to come up and out of her, but she breathed deep, pushed it all back down. She levered herself up off the chair, took the money and slid it into her pocket.

She cleared her throat. "I could take Mason," she said.

"Take some of those damn blocks with you. He'll get too jumpy waiting for you to eat," Gram said and sat back on the couch, reaching for her smokes before her behind had even hit the upholstery.

| | | | |

In the hotel coffee shop Taylor and Mason sat in a booth, Mason's chin level with the edge of the Formica table top, his elbows held high as he lifted a spoon out of his sundae as if out of quicksand. The cooling fudge sauce stretched thin between the bald dome of ice cream and the shallow spoon.

Taylor sat slumped against the orange vinyl seat. When her burger came she tried to make herself eat it, but the texture of the flesh made her gag. Her stomach hurt like hell so she made herself eat some fries, but the salty grease collected around her lips and she suddenly saw the bulbs of yellow fat under Tannis's white skin. Only gulping her Diet Coke in huge swallows kept her from bringing up the half-digested potato. She imagined the cold bubbles sliding down her throat, a mind-over-body sort of thing. It was the same when she was giving Devon a blow job. She knew how to relax her throat and just let it all slide through her, as if it didn't matter.

She felt the cold liquid inside her at first, and then it warmed up and her stomach hurt less.

Mason had made good progress on his scoop of vanilla and was now scraping his spoon against the bottom of the little cup-shaped metal bowl to get the puddled melt. Taylor thought she should try one more time to eat something. She dragged the top bun off her burger and poked the patty with her fork. It broke apart, revealing a jagged gray interior.

Taylor stared at it and imagined that the nubbly gray meat was brain. It was gross to think this way but she couldn't help it. Mason was drinking from a glass of water, holding it with both hands. When he put it down, Taylor stood up and began to collect his blocks, piled near the salt and pepper shakers.

"Let's go upstairs, Macey." She dipped a paper napkin in the water glass and wiped the chocolate smears from his pale face.

As they left the coffee shop, she glanced into the alcove where the pay phones were. A wave of tiredness passed over her. She'd better call Devon. It had been over a day, and he would be mad.

Taylor sat Mason down on the raveled carpet in the corner and let him put his big blocks together and then crack them apart with whooshing explosion sounds. He was too old for these extra-big blocks — they were for little kids — but he didn't have regular Lego so he sometimes played with these. He still liked snapping them together and apart.

Devon's number rang for a long time. Finally his mother answered. Taylor, who had been leaning against the wall staring at the little rips in the wallpaper, regretted calling the moment she heard Kathi Bailey's voice, grogged with sleep and tense with annoyance. Mrs. Bailey worked the night shift at a truckstop off the highway and slept at odd hours. Taylor apologized for waking her, but Devon had Taylor call every day, sometimes more often, and Taylor had woken her too many times.

Taylor heard the phone crack against the tabletop, loud enough to hurt her ear.

Finally Devon came on.

"It's about time," he said. Taylor heard in his voice — low, smooth, controlled — that he was ready to be angry with her but hadn't got there yet.

"I was at the morgue," she said. "I saw Tannis's autopsy."

"Was it disgusting?" His voice was quiet, but a bit eager, too. Taylor hesitated.

"It was my sister's body," she said.

She heard in Devon's breathing that he was thinking. She realized she'd surprised him.

"When are you coming home?" he asked. The image of Tannis's deconstructed corpse still crowded Taylor's mind.

"I don't know. We're going to Gram's tomorrow." Normally she would be telling him she loved him, or missed him. Something to keep his hands from clenching into fists. But right now she was almost too exhausted to talk at all.

There was a tense silence at Devon's end.

"I have to take Mace back to the room now. I'll call you tomorrow as soon as we get back to the house. I promise."

"You better," he said. She knew she'd have to make up her absence with sex next time they saw each other. Nevertheless, she took a deep, easy breath.

| | | | |

It turned out that the move to Gram's was for good. Taylor realized that no one had explained that to her because none of the grownups imagined that she could consider Bracken's house her home. But it was where she'd been living, with Tannis and Mason as her family. Now she felt like a weird refugee.

It was strange walking into Gram's house, stiff from hours in the car, and seeing it not as a place for a holiday visit but knowing they'd be staying there.

Gram and Douglas gave Taylor a little room that had been a sort of pantry. Douglas had pulled the shelves off the wall up to about the level of Taylor's chin so there was room for a cot and a little dresser with three drawers. The wood at the edges of the drawers was splitting, but Gram had lined the insides with blue-flowered adhesive vinyl. There was also a tiny window fused shut by layers of old paint. It kept Taylor from feeling too trapped by the walls during the long mornings and afternoons she spent lying there half-asleep or sitting cross-legged on the cot, her limbs heavy, drinking water from a tall plastic 7-Eleven cup.

She was exhausted, like a drugged animal. She slept a lot. When she was awake she struggled to think through a fog. The short span of days that had started the moment Tannis was dead and ended when Taylor and Mason arrived at Gram's unspooled in her mind's eye like an old movie. She saw herself talking to cops, throwing together clothes for herself and Mason, going to the morgue. It was like watching herself running on some kind of super emergency fuel that kept her moving, drove her to do things she would never normally do. Quiet little Taylor, at the morgue!

And then when she got here, to Gram's, it was like the fuel completely ran out.

Taylor didn't sleep in the pantry at nights, because Mason screamed if he was left to fall asleep by himself. She was tired anyway, so she just went to bed when he did. She took a magazine with her or just sat up against the wall with one arm folded across her stomach and the other one nodding between her mouth and the ashtray. Mason lay diagonally across half of the double bed, his little fists curled and his mouth open, silky bangs scrunched up along his forehead.

Taylor felt all confused and almost dizzy from everything happening so fast. She didn't know why she ever thought she and Mason could just go back to their old house to live.

She didn't know what she would have done with Mason while she was in school, or whether she could have gone back to school at all. And the thought of opening the door one day to find that Bracken had come back was awful. His trial was still months and months away. The police officer had been careful to explain that although Bracken would probably be convicted, no one could say for sure.

Taylor had gotten so used to him hurting Tannis. It seemed normal, like a kid getting a spanking. You saw they didn't like it, but it was okay to hurt them, somehow. But now she was feeling the weight of Tannis's death sink into her own life. Not just that last attack but all the beatings and abuse that led up to it, as if they were all one long killing event. As if Bracken had been taking Tannis away for years, one little piece at a time.

Taylor remembered seeing Bracken slap Tannis, punch Tannis, kick Tannis. When it started, Taylor would just leave. She hated seeing it, but also Tannis used to wave her away. Tannis was embarrassed to be seen being beaten up, and she thought she could handle Bracken better by herself. And Taylor remembered Tannis lifting her shining face to Bracken's when things were good. At those times it was easy to believe the other stuff didn't matter.

Now Taylor would never see Tannis again, ever. Every time she realized that, it took a minute for her to adjust, and then the knowledge sank onto her like concrete.

The new life wasn't all bad, though. She loved Devon but she'd been beginning to feel stuck with him, had begun to gaze jealously at the dork girls with no boyfriends. The constant gnawing fear — would he be mad if she said this, would he hate it if she wore that — had been wearing her down. Now she lived far enough away that he couldn't blame her if she didn't have money for the long bus trip. And Douglas was firm about restricting long-distance calls. Taylor worried about Devon getting mad at her for not calling enough, and she'd pleaded with Douglas, but he wouldn't budge.

One evening he took the phone right out of her hand.

"This is my house. These are my rules," Douglas said into the phone. Taylor heard Devon say "Yes, sir" on the other end, just like he was talking to his dad.

Taylor kind of hoped Devon would get bored waiting for her. She knew he could easily find another girl to keep his big hand on. Small and alone as she felt, she told herself she had to think of her future now — hers and Mason's. At first she thought of Devon so often, missed his smell, the small hairs at the back of his neck. Now each day he seemed farther away.

Maybe it was better like this.

After two weeks Gram came to the door of the little pantry. She folded an arm across her blouse, smoke from her cigarette curling into the hair at her temple.

Taylor could tell this would be bad news. Normally Gram was all business, which came across as brusque un- til you knew her. Really it was just Gram's way of packing two days of work, housecleaning and errands into every day, running on four or five hours of sleep, two packs of cigs and a variety of caffeinated drinks. Gram drove a school bus morning and afternoon, and also answered the phone in an office from 9 a.m. to 2:30 in the afternoon when she had to leave to pick the kids up. All the housework got done before or after that. Taylor had learned early on to take Gram's affection the way it came — in the form of hot meals, clean floors and folded laundry.

The social worker had phoned Gram to say that Taylor had to start at her new school on Monday, no more delays. Mason had already started, climbing the steps of the school bus in the mornings with his new backpack hunched over his nylon windbreaker, hauling his little feet all the way up to the grooved rubber mat on the first step of the bus.

Taylor met him after school, standing apart from the moms at the corner waiting for the little kids to be released from their big yellow can on wheels. She huddled in her sweatshirt in the October wind. She didn't have a winter coat. Tannis had given her a new white quilted ski jacket for Christmas the year before, but Devon got mad at her in February and burnt it with his lighter.

Looking up at Gram's stern face, Taylor knew she wouldn't stand for any fooling around. She was kind of surprised, actually, that Gram had let her get away with lying around the house for so long.

Taylor had stayed with Gram the summer after her mom died, too. It seemed forever ago, when she was twelve. The following September Tannis and Mason moved in with Bracken, and Taylor went to live with them so she could stay in her regular school.

Taylor's strongest memory of the time right after her mom's death was Gram cooking and cleaning the house like crazy. The bathrooms stank so badly of bleach that it made Taylor's eyes water when she went in to take a pee. Gram had cooked constantly, starting after the police found Virginia slumped over the wheel of her old Malibu and continuing until several days after the funeral. They had so much meat in the house — roast beef, ham — that Gram and Taylor packed up Baggies full of it and gave them out to anyone who came in.

When the autopsy report showed Virginia had died of a heart attack and not, as the police had suggested, from an accident caused by driving drunk, Gram went out and cleaned the gutters all on her own. When she came back in in her black rubber boots and made herself a cup of tea with milk and sugar and just sat quiet at the kitchen table for a while, Taylor knew she'd passed some stage in her grieving, and after that it all began to get back to something like normal.

Now Gram stood, silent, in Taylor's doorway.

"Okay," Taylor said. Maybe she would find a new boyfriend in this new school. A boy who wasn't quite so hard on her as Devon.

Gram fingered a folded-up wad of paper from her cardigan pocket and pressed it into Taylor's hand.

"You better go get whatever you need — notebooks, a winter coat," Gram said, her voice a little unsteady. "I can't have them saying I can't take care of you."

Taylor knew this wasn't about what anybody else thought. She stood up and hugged Gram quick around her shoulders, and as soon as she let go, Gram was already halfway turned around and out the door.

"That's half your Christmas right there, I'm sorry to say," she muttered over her shoulder, and Taylor had to smile, her thumb pushing apart the pleated bills so she could feel the thickness of the layers. She figured there was two hundred dollars here. That was probably most of Gram's Christmas money for all of them.

Gram drove her to the mall after supper and went to Tim Hortons for a coffee while Taylor drifted through the stores.

She was focusing on a winter jacket. She'd been through four stores without trying anything on when she realized she was unconsciously looking for the same white ski jacket Devon burned up last year. She had to stop in front of a shoe store to close her eyes and wait for a sort of dizziness to pass.

Finally she turned into the next store with winter coats, determined to buy something different.

Everything was too expensive until, in the back of a store, she found a rack of coats on sale. She slid them along the pole one by one. There was a nice burgundy wool that faded to purple toward the hem and cuffs, and had soft knotted fringes. She pulled it out to try it on and found herself staring through the gap in the coats at a girl about her age.

The girl had light brown eyes in a pale face under violet-streaked bangs. Her long fingers were emerging from the sleeve of another one of the same coat, which matched her purple hair. The girl was taller than Taylor and the coat was too short for her. Her wrists cleared the cuffs with an inch or so to spare.

She looked up and saw Taylor and smiled.

"It's a nice coat," she said, hanging it back on the rack. "One of these should fit you. I'm such a giraffe," she whispered. "I need, like, a super-maxi-length or something." She winked, then turned and walked out of the store.

Taylor stood for a moment watching the girl go. Her simple unexpected friendliness made Taylor's heart hurt.

The only friends she had at home were the girlfriends of Devon's friends, which is why he trusted her with them. She mostly saw them at school or out in a group with Devon. They never went shopping or hung out on their own.

Taylor stood looking at the empty doorway of the store. The tall girl had disappeared.

Finally she turned back to the rack and tried on the coat. It fit perfectly. Taylor looked at herself in the narrow mirror mounted on the wall behind her and felt warm. She turned the wide collar up so it framed her face in a cloud of soft burgundy, giving her pale skin some color, some life.

|||||

At the new school, feeling stiff in her new boots and coat, a messenger bag with a ring binder and books inside, Taylor let herself be a rock, let the stream of new faces and names and classrooms wash over her.

At lunchtime she ate by herself, an egg-salad sandwich and a Diet Coke from the machine. Afterward she went outside to have a cigarette, keeping to herself. She worried briefly about Mason, now being picked up by one of the corner moms who would keep him with her own kid until Taylor got home.

After lunch she had biology. It was so different from the class at her old school. She hardly understood anything. At the end of the day she fairly burst from the school building, stopping only long enough to light a cigarette in the lee of the doorway before charging down the sidewalk and off to the bus stop, her book bag banging against her hip with each step. Her new boots jarred on the concrete sidewalk.

At the mom's house, Mason appeared in the doorway,

the woman helping him with his jacket. He stood, resigned as an old pony, as she adjusted the straps of his backpack. He had a red bruise on his cheek and a crust of dried milk on his upper lip, and when his jacket was all Velcroed closed he dove out the door and down the walk, slipping his hand into Taylor's as he passed.

They walked as fast as they could up the block to Gram's, and as soon as they got in the door, Taylor kicked it shut and then sat straight down onto the floor and let Mason collapse into the well of her open knees. She hugged him, her nose buried in the fine Mason-smelling hair at the back of his head, his little arms hooked up over Taylor's like a baby monkey's.

|||||

Over the weeks, they developed a routine. Gram got up at five and made Douglas's breakfast and packed everyone's lunches, a clutch of sandwiches appearing like doves between the hands of a magician — granola bars, apples, a Thermos of hot coffee slotted into the row of lunch boxes and paper bags. By the time Taylor had her shower and got herself and Mason dressed, Douglas was off and Gram had set up another round of breakfast. Taylor washed the dishes and wiped the counter after Gram headed out the door to get her bus warmed up, and then she walked Mason to his bus and then on to school herself. If there were no hitches, if Mason's bus wasn't late, then Taylor arrived at school just in time to have a smoke outside and slip into her seat in geometry before the second bell.

At the end of the day they did the whole thing sort of backwards, Taylor picking Mason up at the mom's house and getting home in time to peel potatoes. After they ate, Gram did the washing up, then installed herself at the kitchen table with a last cup of coffee before she went to do laundry or some other task.

Sometimes Taylor would glance up from her homework and catch a glimpse of Gram at rest for a moment. Her face was like a dried riverbed, lined with shadows. Taylor knew fifty wasn't that old — Madonna was almost fifty — but Gram's life had been hard on her. Taylor wondered whether she would look like that one day, too.

Devon called a couple of times a week. He wanted to know about her new school. Did she have any new friends?

"Come on, Tay," he said, "you must be meeting people in your classes."

"They all know each other already. It's not like at the beginning of the year when lots of people are new."

"Come on, Tay, don't give me that shit." His voice jokey. If he was here he'd throw his arm over her shoulders and grin. "Don't tell me you haven't met anyone. There are a lot of guys in your school, aren't there?"

He interrogated her about every detail of her school day. Taylor felt herself disappearing as he tried to see past her.

"Who do you eat lunch with?"

"No one."

"Who do you sit with in the cafeteria?"

"I don't even go in there some days. I just eat my sand-wiches Gram makes me."

"Come on. Haven't you met anybody?"

"Not really."

"It's a yes or no question, stupid. If you're not saying no then it must be yes."

"No. The answer's no. I haven't made any friends."

"Come on, Tay, what are you hiding? Are you seeing someone?"

"No, Dev, I love you. I'm not seeing anybody. I don't know anybody. I promise." He was quiet. She could hear him inhaling, then blowing out smoke.

"When I come see you, you're gonna have to introduce me to your friends," he said.

"Dev, I don't have any. When you come I'll just want to see you. I miss you."

There was a long silence. She knew what was coming.

"You're such a bitch, Tay! You go off and leave me, and there you are in a new school with new friends and I'm still here all by myself!" Her chin was on her chest now, the phone loose in her hand. She could hear that he was gritting his back teeth. "You better not be lying to me!"

It relieved her to be able to tell Devon truthfully that she didn't have any friends. She knew it would make him feel better, even if he didn't believe her.

Before, Taylor was with Devon all the time. Now, at school and on the street, she was teaching herself the habits of the lonely. The glazed eyes that didn't make contact but didn't appear to be avoiding anyone, the bolt from any crowded room and the quick walk that made her look too busy to stop and chat. The focused attention on a sandwich that made it seem that she didn't even realize she was eating alone.

It was just as well. It wasn't as if she could hang around with anyone outside of school, since she had Mason to look after. If she had new friends, maybe even a new boyfriend, she would want to turn her attention to her new life. She couldn't keep managing the relationship with Devon at this distance. He'd get another girlfriend — if he didn't have one already. Hopefully by the time Taylor was ready to make a break, their relationship would have faded away anyway. Otherwise Devon would be raging mad about it, and she wouldn't dare.

After a few weeks Taylor recognized more of the faces in her classes. In geometry she usually ended up next to a long-haired boy whose notebook said *Woo* on the front. In English she was assigned to work on a project with a girl named Tiffany, but since she couldn't stay after school to meet in the library they just planned it on the phone and each did one part separately.

On Halloween Taylor felt especially lonely, as students in costumes wandered the halls, trading candy or making party plans.

She and Devon had had their first kiss on Halloween two years ago. They'd been flirting since the school year started, and he'd finally broken up with his previous girlfriend that morning. He made sure Taylor knew about it, passing the word through a kid in her English class.

Taylor had dressed as a fairy, with plastic wings and silver leggings. She took Mason, in a Dollar Store firefighter costume, trick-or-treating around the block. When they returned she saw that their neighbors had made a haunted house, so Taylor took Mason home and then went to the haunted house on her own. A dark hallway was hung with drapes and lit by glow-in-the-dark skull faces. A soundtrack of ghostly moans played in the background. To pass down the hallway she had to stick her hands into bowls of gummi candy worms and uncooked-sausage guts. When she plunged her hand into the bowl of peeled-grape eyeballs, she felt someone grab her wrist and pull her back behind the drapes. She thought it was part of the haunted house until she felt the person gently lift her chin and tenderly kiss her, just for a moment. She gasped, and he pulled her close and whispered in her ear, "Don't be scared. It's me, Devon." Then he kissed her again, longer and warmer, and she sank into his chest and gave herself to the smell of his breath and his hair gel and the rough pads on the palms of his hands, as kids on the other side of the curtain squealed and shrieked just inches away from them.

So much had changed since then. Taylor couldn't keep her mind on anything. In biology, which Mr. Assouad taught wearing a plastic glasses-nose-and-mustache, she completely blew the pop quiz and then, handing in her half-empty paper, knocked over the teacher's cup full of pencils and pens. They crashed to the floor and rolled all over and Taylor scrambled to pick them up, her face hot. As soon as she'd jammed them all back into the cup, she grabbed her coat, pushed her way through the crowd of students in the doorway and made a beeline outside to light a smoke. She fumbled with her lighter, wishing she could just disappear.

She inhaled deeply several times, feeling the rush of hot smoke begin to ease into her blood, when a tap on her shoulder made her jump so hard she nearly hit the back of her head against the concrete wall behind her. Standing next to her was Woo, wearing a plastic Viking helmet, offering her a joint. Beyond him were a couple of kids she recognized as stoners, including, she realized with a jolt, the girl who had tried on her coat at the mall.

The coat girl was looking at her, head cocked in a friendly, curious way, and Taylor felt self-conscious. She took the joint and took a big lovely hit off it, then got to her feet and muttered thanks, but that she had to go. All she could think of doing was to bolt for the bus stop. She ended up walking the whole way home, her lungs aching with every breath, her cheeks blown bright red and cold by the Halloween wind.

Two

LILY'S EARLIEST MEMORY was of screaming with happiness.

She was flying. Her heart was sliding up inside her and it felt so good. Her father was throwing her up in the air and catching her again. She remembered this from inside her chest — the feeling of flying, the thrill shooting through her limbs and blooming out to the ends of her fingers and toes.

She had no memory at all of the story her mother often told, of the way Lily slipped through her father's hands and crashed to the floor, arm crumpled under her, screaming now from shock and pain. Her mother described her father huffing his stinky breath as he struggled to pick her up, her way of saying he was drunk without actually saying it. (That perfume of beer, moist and warm, used to be a happy smell for Lily — he was most affectionate when he'd had a few.) Her mother told how she pulled her away from him and ran with her to the car, laying Lily across the back seat and peeling out to the Emergency room. Her mother reaching into the back to lay a hand on Lily's stomach for comfort as Lily screamed all the way there.

Telling this story, her mother identified this incident as the beginning of the end of their marriage.

Sometimes, coming home stoned from Jay Woo's house and lying in her dark bedroom eating cheese popcorn from a bag on her chest, Lily wondered whether it had even happened. She had vague memories of her cast — gray and ragged — with threads leaking out around the edges of the openings where her knuckles and her thumb stuck out.

Her mother never said as much, but the way she referred to him bitterly as "your father" made Lily feel she was somehow responsible for him.

And clearly, if she was responsible, she'd failed.

She felt guilty for doubting her mother's story, guilty for believing it.

Her father's story about the breakup was of Lily's mother's car accident, her brain injury, the time she spent in the rehab place. The way her personality changed.

Lily's mother got furious when she overheard him telling that story to his family the Christmas Lily was seven and got a Barbie Dream House under the tree at Nana's. Lily's mother said "fuck you" to Lily's father. They had a yelling fight in front of everyone, and Lily's mother spat in his face, which still shocked Lily. Then she pulled Lily out the door without even giving her time to put her arms into the sleeves of her coat.

Lily didn't get to see her Barbie Dream House again for a long time, until one day she came home and Uncle

Gil was parked in front of the apartment building. He slid the Dream House out of the back seat, putting his finger in front of his mouth, shhh. He carried it inside and put it down in front of the apartment door, then grinned and winked, disappearing back down the stairs.

Maybe it was the way her mother's face closed up when she saw Lily dragging it in through the door, but the Dream House wasn't that fun afterward. She never played with it much.

She did play with the Barbie she found stuck inside — legs scissored open and arms rigid, like Barbie was doing a robot walk. She experimented with slamming the kitchen drawers shut on Barbie's limbs; they didn't break. She drew on them with black marker pens until Barbie's legs and arms were covered in smudged ink. She cut off Barbie's hair — just the ends at first, then shorter and shorter until she ended up gouging Barbie's skull with the point of the scissors. She dipped Barbie's scraggly, almost-bald head in the toilet, but her makeup never smeared.

Lily was used to seeing her mother's makeup smudged on her tired face after a long day at her crappy job at the workshop for people with disabilities, or after a date, or when she had drunk a tall gin and tonic alone in the kitchen, listening to the radio. Lily once summoned all her courage and asked her mother not to drink those tall drinks anymore. She thought her mother would be angry. Instead, her mother just looked at her for a minute, then leaned forward and stroked Lily's face. "Mommy has to have a drink sometimes, honey." Since the car accident, she explained, she sometimes had pains in her head that only a drink could help.

A girl's gotta do what a girl's gotta do, as Uncle Gil used to say.

Lily knew about the pains. She often rubbed her mother's temples. Until she got tall enough, she stood on a chair behind her mother's chair to reach. Or she brought her mother cold washcloths for her forehead while she lay in bed waiting for her pills to "kick in." Lily stood by the bed, mouse-quiet, imagining little legs and feet kicking her poor mother's head from the inside.

The car accident happened when Lily was still little — after the broken arm, but before she could remember much. So she didn't have any idea whether her mother really changed. There were things her mother did that Lily knew were brain-injury things. Like when she put the pot on the stove and the lid on the pot, and then poured the dry rice onto the lid so it scattered all over the stove and bounced onto the floor.

Or when she picked up a spoon and tried to use it to sign Lily's museum field trip permission slip. She'd look up at Lily, a crooked grin on her face. She knew she was using the wrong utensil, but her brain couldn't figure out why. She'd knit her brow, concentrate, then turn the spoon around and try to sign with the handle end.

Sometimes, when her mother had mean boyfriends who hit her, Lily wondered if they were injuring her brain more. She'd keep an eye out, checking to see if her mother became more retarded, or started acting weirder. These bouts were often followed by days of sunglasses and ice packs, or wailing days. Either way Lily knew she would have to do everything by herself. Get up for school and get her own cereal, heat up cans of soup for supper for both of them when she came home. If it lasted a long time she would wash some underwear and T-shirts in dish detergent in the bathroom sink to have clothes to wear to school.

But she never saw a personality change she could put her finger on. Her mother could be abrupt and unreasonable, and when she'd been drinking she could be embarrassing around men — loud and flirty, laughing too much.

But then, a lot of kids' parents were like that.

Three

A FEW DAYS AFTER Halloween, at the beginning of biology, the stoner girl dropped into the desk on the other side of Taylor and introduced herself, raising her voice over the noise of notebooks flipping open and papers being shuffled. Taylor was so good at keeping her gaze to herself that she had never even noticed the girl in the crowded classroom.

Today she was wearing a necklace made of linked-together pull-tabs. Devon would have said it looked trashy, but Taylor kind of liked it. Beer, she wondered, or maybe Coke?

The girl's name was Lily. The name suited her pale skin and straight dark hair, half her bangs still purple. She looked like a cut flower, the creamy light of her face perfect for reflecting in water.

She dumped her backpack on the floor and then, leaning away from Taylor to dip into it, she turned her face up and smiled. Jutting her chin toward the back of Taylor's chair, she said, "Nice coat," before turning her attention to the front of the room.

The next day Taylor was standing at the Coke machine waiting for her can to thump into the trough when she felt someone standing right at her back. Immediately she saw Devon in her mind's eye, and her breath caught.

There stood Lily, smiling a small restrained smile.

"No worries," Lily said quietly. "Just me."

Taylor felt transparent. Lily had looked right into her, but strangely enough, Taylor didn't mind.

"Shall we dine?" Lily asked, cocking her head toward the entrance to the caf.

After that Lily found her every day. She fell into step beside Taylor in the hallways, appeared behind her in the caf, headed off to smoke after lunch as if she expected Taylor to follow. Taylor was afraid to count on Lily being there, but in spite of herself she got used to it, got used to Lily's greeting of "Nice coat," got used to Lily's small smile on her long face. Got used to Lily never asking her why she had to take off right after school.

This, Taylor knew, was the sign of a girl who had baggage of her own.

So it was a surprise when details about their lives popped out. Like the day they were leaving the caf and a boy sitting at the end of a table grabbed Taylor's ass as she walked past.

She batted his hand away. "Don't touch me, asshole." The boys laughed.

"Don't call me asshole, slut!" the groper said loudly, grinning at the other boys. Taylor felt shrunk to a hard nub, but she was with Lily, so she gathered her courage.

"Don't call me slut, asshole!"

"You're a slut, and your mother's a slut," he replied.

Taylor whirled on him. "My mother's dead!" she screamed, then ran. She wedged herself into a corner under the stairs and buried her face in her hands, sobbing, wanting the whole world to go away.

When she finally raised her head, Lily was there.

"Good comeback," Lily said.

Taylor shook her head. "It's true. She had a heart attack and crashed her car."

Lily nodded. "My mom was in a car accident, too. She didn't die, but it smashed up her brain." She shrugged. "She's kind of retarded now."

"Fuck off!" Taylor said, her eyes wide.

"No, it's really true. She tried to put her feet in the arms of her sweater this morning. She couldn't figure out why it only came up to her butt-cheeks."

They looked at each other and began to laugh. The bell rang and they got up and walked down the hall, leaning on each other and trying to stifle their giggles before they got to biology.

With Lily, Taylor began to feel more at ease with the stoner kids. She got used to calling the boy she thought of as "Woo" Jay instead, like his friends. Half-belonging to the stoner crowd, although she wasn't exactly friends with anyone but Lily, she was no longer an orphan in the social world of the school. Having someone to share biology notes with didn't hurt, either.

But even as school got a little easier thanks to Lily, Taylor still had her bad moments.

One evening the phone rang. Taylor grabbed it and got a little shock when she recognized Devon's voice.

"Dev," she said. "I...wasn't expecting you."

"Why? Is someone there with you?" His voice was suddenly hard.

"No, no one. I mean, just Mason. I'm folding laundry." It was true, but she also liked the idea of Devon picturing her safe at home, doing some household thing.

But it was too late.

"You're lying, you bitch. Who is it?"

"No, no one, I promise."

"If I find out you are, you won't recognize yourself in a mirror when I'm through with you."

"I promise, baby," she said softly. Her heart was pounding slowly inside her chest. Mason was standing by the fridge sipping fruit punch, and she tried to get his attention. She flapped her hand at him and pointed toward the kitchen door, but he ignored her.

"One day you'll turn around and I'll be there. You won't know what hit you," Devon said.

"Dev..." Taylor began, and then Mason cried out as his cup tumbled out of his hands, spilling fruit punch on the sheets Taylor had just washed and folded.

Rage tore through her. She leaped up and hit the side of his little head with the handset. He gasped, and the terrible look of fear that crossed his face pierced her heart.

That night in Mason's room, his breathing interrupted by occasional wet coughs in the bed beside her, Taylor remembered when Bracken hit Tannis in the face with the portable phone.

Devon and Taylor were supposed to go to a movie, and he was coming to pick her up. Her purse was in the kitchen where Bracken and Tannis were fighting, and she was waiting and waiting for a chance to get it. She had to be ready to run out when she heard Devon drive up.

Finally there was a lull in the shouting and she took a chance. But she walked in just as Bracken took a great big swing and smashed the hard plastic right into the middle of Tannis's face. Taylor heard the awful hollow crunch and then, like a bottle of champagne popping open, the blood fountained up and sprayed in all directions.

Bracken threw the phone into the kitchen sink and stormed out the front door. Taylor emptied an ice tray into a dish towel and held it against Tannis's uptilted face while with the other hand she reached into the sink for the phone to call 911. As the dial tone came through, she heard Devon beep his horn outside and at the same time heard the gurgling as Tannis began to choke on the blood pouring down her throat.

What Taylor had remembered about that night until now was that Devon held her while she calmed down. Then, angry that Taylor had to stay home with a sleeping Mason while Tannis went to the hospital, he had beaten her from wrist to shoulder on both arms and forced her to give him a blow job right there in the living room. With her nose clogged from crying and her arms hurting so much she thought maybe they were broken, she'd knelt before Devon and worked to bring him off, all the while straining to listen, praying that Mason wouldn't wake up and that neither Bracken nor Tannis would come home before Devon filled the back of Taylor's throat.

When he loosened his grip on her hair and bent to kiss the top of her head, the flood of relief and gratitude totally washed away the icky feeling of him lying on her tongue like a giant warm slug.

Now she remembered the way Tannis's nose was squashed and the cartilage underneath collapsed. And in her mind she heard the knocking sound of Gram's phone bouncing ever so slightly against Mason's little round skull, and she saw his look of stunned fear. It tore at her, made a river of pain right down to her stomach.

. |||||

Taylor knew Lily was really her friend when she found herself telling Devon about her on the phone. It was a calculated risk. Better for him not to know she had other friends. He'd be jealous, plus it would make him start thinking she was seeing other boys. But if he found out later that she'd hidden Lily from him, it would be bad. She played down Lily's importance in her life, which was easy since she did it for herself, too, letting Devon believe that she was stringing Lily along for the sake of her biology grade.

She heard Devon pause on the other end of the phone. If he was closer Taylor could sleep with him, rub his back, make him bacon sandwiches. She knew this stuff made him less tense. Not that she wouldn't have liked to rub his back, have sex with him — she imagined him kissing her neck and it made her smile and close her eyes for a moment to hold the memory. She was beginning to miss all that, now that she was sort of waking up again, coming back to herself in this new place. She missed his smell.

Taylor and Lily hung out often enough that the other kids knew they were friends, but since Taylor had to go home right after school, they never saw each other outside of classes. They didn't have much chance to talk alone face to face unless they happened to be having a cigarette outside before any other kids came out. As winter came on, everyone ended up huddling inside the same doorway.

At first Taylor thought Lily might be wary about being friends with the new kid, but after a few doorway smokes, she realized Lily honestly didn't care. She was quietly friendly with everyone. After they ground their butts into the dirty snow, she'd throw a lanky arm around Taylor's neck and the two of them would crunch out into the schoolyard.

Taylor wondered about bringing Lily home to hang out in the hour before supper, but she already felt like an intruder at Gram's. Douglas was usually napping when Taylor and Mason got home, but not always. He was not exactly unfriendly, but he didn't talk to them much, and Taylor tried hard not to be in the way.

Nevertheless, when Lily asked her to come out to the library one night to study, Taylor bundled Mason into his snowsuit and took him with her, setting him at the end of the table with a pile of picture books from the kids' section and a contraband box of Smarties, a gift from Lily. Living with Bracken, he had developed an almost unnatural ability to play quietly on his own, and he slipped into that now as Taylor and Lily whispered into their books across the library table.

Taylor pulled a hand-drawn diagram of the developing human embryo — from single cell to blastocyst — from her bag.

"Due tomorrow. Start it yet?" she asked Lily in a low voice.

Lily looked surprised. "No! When did you do that?"

Taylor grinned. "Spare period. I heard you tell Jay you didn't do it yet. Copy mine."

"You rock!" Lily whispered loudly, leaning over to slap Taylor's shoulder. Taylor couldn't stop smiling.

As they sat there, Lily sometimes leaned over and whispered to Mason. Now and then he slid a Smartie over to her and grinned when, without looking up, she slid it back to him.

After that Taylor phoned Lily quickly every day when she got home from school, if Douglas was sleeping.

"Hey, Lily-liver, how you doing?"

"Fine, T-Bone. My mom actually went grocery shopping — hambooger helper tonight. How you?"

"Fine. Hamboogers here, too — no helper."

Taylor, grinding out her last cig after school one afternoon, heard Lily telling Jay she couldn't come over until later, if at all. He didn't reply, but his face got hard. Taylor had seen this expression on Devon, and it made her freeze. But Lily flashed Jay a sideways smile and, as she turned away, grazed his arm with a goofy punch. He grinned sheepishly and hit her back with an elbow.

Taylor admired Lily for standing up to this boy. He wasn't her boyfriend, but if there was a boy in her orbit it was him.

Four

LILY HAD NEVER HAD a boyfriend. No wonder, with her giraffe-girl powers of tallness and skinniness. She and Jay Woo had made out a couple of times, when they were the only ones in his basement and they thought, with stoned logic, that they should just give it a try.

The kissing was okay. Weird, though. Weird to be touching the inside of another person's mouth, where they made spit and chewed food.

It was kind of nice to be so close and quiet and warm with Jay. She liked his long glossy hair and his smooth skin. He loved to smoke dope and hang around the stoners, but Lily knew he was also really good at drawing and knew a lot about different things, especially weather.

He told her about it the first time they kissed. They'd been tentatively touching lips, their hands brushing each other, and then they just sat for a while. They didn't turn on any lights. They sat on the couch in a nest of gathering darkness, and he told her he wanted to be a meteorologist.

At first she thought that was like astronomy, that it was about meteors, but he explained that it was someone who studied the weather. He told her the Korean spelling of his name was Jae.

The second time they kissed, she even unbuttoned her shirt for him when he tried to slip his hand inside. He gazed at her white bra and then reached out and squeezed one of her breasts — not hard, but it surprised her, and she pulled away. She immediately wished she hadn't, but it was too late. They looked away from each other and then she rebuttoned her shirt, and they went and sat on opposite ends of the couch and pretended to watch cartoons.

Not having a boyfriend was part of Lily being a freak. Living in subsidized housing with a freak mother, being a giraffe girl. Staying up until 2 a.m. to finish *Wuthering Heights* because it was so amazing, then going to English class the next day to hear the other kids moan about how deadly boring it was. Her purple bangs waved in the breeze like a flag — a sign that she had surrendered to her freak status.

Plus it didn't seem fair that with all this inner freakness, Lily's mother added so much weirdness to her life. Lily hated the way her mother's brain made them live.

So Lily had to sweep up spilled rice. Okay. Moderately normal. She also had to go with her mother to the doctor and the dentist and explain things for her, make sure she took her pills every day, take her mother to buy groceries right away when she got her check from work so she didn't accidentally blow the food money on beer or a lifetime supply of Styrofoam coffee cups, like she did once. Not very normal. There were days when she wanted to ditch her mother in the canned soup aisle and just walk out of the store and be free. But okay. A girl with an abnormal mother had to do what a girl had to do.

But why did her mother have to bring home those assholes?

"I like them," her mother said.

"You like when they hit you and call you names?"

Her mother looked away. "No, but I like when they ..." She struggled to find a word. "N-nice," she said finally.

"How often are they nice?"

Her mother was red-faced. "You shuts up, Lily. You not nice now."

"C'mon, Mom," Lily insisted loudly. Her mother shrank a little on the couch as Lily loomed over her from the middle of the room. "How often are they nice?"

Her mother looked down at her hands.

"How often?" Lily yelled.

Her mother, mouth set, refused to look at her.

She knew her mother had no answer. If she, Lily, was a freak, her mother was a double freak. A double-triple freak. So she had to take what she could get.

Lily hated the world sometimes.

In the silence, her mother's face was closed and dull. Lily could see why someone would want to punch it. She hated her mother sometimes, too.

"You. Are. Retarded!" Lily shouted. She whirled around, grabbed her coat from the hook by the door and stomped out, slamming the door as hard as she could, knowing it would hurt her mother's head.

Five

By the end of November Mason started spending some afternoons and the occasional weekend night at his new friend Trevor's house. Trevor was a quiet kid with a strange hesitation in his speech. It took him longer to make friends, but when he did he held fast. Mason tended to get frustrated and hit and yell, but Trevor had an uncanny ability to gentle him, like a good rider with a nervous horse.

Taylor immediately began to spend more time with Lily and even, sometimes, an hour in Jay's basement. She made sure she got home in time to start supper for Gram, sometimes throw a load of clothes in the wash. She still had days when it was like a vast iron slab weighed on her head and shoulders. But the routine of school kept her putting one foot in front of the other. She still had afternoons when she just lay in her pantry bed smoking cigarettes, but they were fewer and farther between.

Devon, on the other hand, demanded that Taylor come visit him.

"Dev, I can't. Gram won't let me. Douglas won't let me."

"What a bunch of bullshit. You're seeing someone, aren't you?"

"No, Dev, I swear, I'm not seeing anyone. Swear swear swear. I can't come because Gram and Douglas won't let me. Plus I have to be here to take care of Mason. Gram and Douglas are both at work in the daytime."

"You're full of shit, Tay. You just don't want to see me."

"Dev, I do! I can't leave Mason alone, he's only six. And anyway I don't have any money for the bus. I have no way to get there."

"Get some money from your grandma."

"I can't, she doesn't have any. She already has to take care of us."

"Tell her it's important." His voice was getting lower.

"I can't," Taylor said, her throat tight. She knew Devon could usually beg or steal a few dollars from his mother if he really needed it. She was a waitress and often had a pile of tips on her dresser. But Douglas managed all the money in this house, giving Gram a budget for groceries and gas. Once she squirreled Christmas and birthday money out of it, there was nothing left.

"Just go in her purse and take it."

Taylor heard the slow heat in his voice.

"You don't want to keep me waiting, bitch," Devon said, his voice going even lower. "I'll give you such a smack. If I find out you're fucking some faggot there I'll pound the shit out of you. What's the matter, don't you love me?" His voice was getting higher again. "Don't you miss me? I miss you so much, Tay! If you loved me as much as I love you, you'd want to be here with me."

"I do love you," Taylor said. "I love you, Dev."

"I should come out there and teach you a lesson. I have needs, you know. Maybe you don't, but I do. Don't make me come out there and show you, bitch. You'll fuckin' regret it, I promise. If you loved me you wouldn't make me do this, Tay."

"I do," Taylor repeated. "I love you, I do love you. I love you." Taylor's voice got so hoarse it squeaked.

"Show me," Devon said, his voice so quiet it really scared Taylor.

"I will," she whispered, and she hung up and went and pleaded with Douglas for permission and bus fare. When he was unmoving, she begged Gram. Gram just shook her head, mashing Miracle Whip into a bowl of tuna flakes for sandwiches. Taylor asked Gram if she could go back for Christmas.

Gram leaned on the counter and cocked her head at Taylor. "And where would you stay?" she asked.

Taylor stared at Gram. After a few seconds she whispered, "At our house?" and even as she was saying it she didn't want to hear the answer, didn't want to see the giant black hole that she had pulled open with her bare hands.

"You can't go there, honey. It's Bracken's house." Gram turned back to the tuna salad. "He's in jail, but the house is his."

Taylor looked away, biting her lip.

When she told Devon on the phone that she definitely couldn't come, he got very quiet. Taylor didn't know how to read this uncharacteristic silence, but it frightened her.

|||||

The day they got back their biology labs — Taylor's with a big, unexpected, highest-ever red 74% scrawled across the top — she and Lily bumped hips in the hall after class, and Taylor had a tiny moment of simple happiness. When school ended, Lily met her outside to walk over to Jay's house. Lily passed Taylor her Diet Coke, and when it washed into her mouth, Taylor realized that it was spiked with rum. Lily winked at her and smiled, and even though she didn't like rum, Taylor had another swig just to celebrate.

In Jay's basement they sat hip to hip on an old corduroy beanbag chair while Jay and a couple of other guys listened to music and tried to play stoned Hacky Sack. Lily pulled a bottle of black nail polish out of her bag, picked up Taylor's hand and started to paint her fingernails. Taylor tried to pull away, but Lily didn't let go.

Lily looked up at her, smiling with her eyes. "Just for fun?" she said softly. It made Taylor feel so warm she couldn't say no.

When her nails were dry (and she had to admit they looked cool), she took Lily's hand. As she was doing Lily's right thumb, one of the boys launched the Hacky Sack at them and almost knocked over the polish. Taylor whipped around, but before she could yell anything, Lily, laughing, said, "Fuck off," and threw the Hacky Sack back at them.

Taylor was amazed. She found herself stroking her anger smaller and smaller until it disappeared completely. It was like a magic trick — like Lily had shown her a little magic.

She looked up and wondered whether she could touch

Lily's long throat some time, or maybe just behind her ear where she had a tattoo of a skull enfolded by a long-petaled lily, mostly hidden behind the shadows of her hair.

After that Taylor watched Lily. She saw that Lily was good at finding a way to be funny with people instead of blowing up at them. She got them to chill out. Taylor wanted to know how to do that.

Lily sometimes threw her long arm over Taylor's shoulder in the hallways, or poked Jay in the ribs, not caring who saw them. And Taylor's biology grades stayed up. Now that she was feeling like she could, she really wanted to do well.

She began to relax so much that when she picked up the phone at the beginning of December, she was shocked to feel her whole body clench at the sound of Devon's voice.

"You better stop fucking avoiding me," he said, his voice low.

Taylor heard her voice high and pushing tears. "I'm not avoiding you. I want to see you, I just can't. Gram and Douglas said no."

Devon's voice suddenly switched to warm caramel. "You love me, don't you, Tay?"

Taylor still felt a thrill when he spoke to her that way. She had never had a boyfriend before Devon, and before Tannis died and they moved, she often imagined marrying him. He was blunt and clean to look at, and would work in his father's garage when he finished school. He even had plans to expand the business, maybe have a dealership one day.

"Yes," she whispered, and part of her meant it even while the new part of her stood a few steps to the side, shaking her head.

"You're not avoiding me?"

"No." She knew that even though his voice still sounded nice, he was angry, and it scared her when it was hidden like this. "Douglas said I can't go on the bus, and he won't let Gram take me. They want me to stay and work on school stuff. Plus I have to take care of Mason."

"I miss you, Tay," he said resentfully. "It's totally boring here. School sucks. I'm grounded from going out for a week, for no reason." He paused. "Alls I did was, I fired an empty bottle at that fat security guard at the hockey rink. And there's nothing on TV. My dad's being a complete asshole. It was empty. Nobody even got hurt."

"Sorry, baby." Taylor knew this meant his father was furious with him. The first time she ever went to Devon's house, they laid their bikes on the driveway and went inside. They were drinking Cokes in the kitchen when they heard Devon's dad bellowing.

"Devon! Get out here, you little piece of shit, and move these piles of junk!" Devon's face turned white, and he was off his stool and out the door faster than Taylor had ever seen anyone move. She followed, feeling guilty for leaving her bike out, too. She got outside just in time to see Devon's father, in the driver's seat of his pickup, holding Devon by the hair through the open truck window. Devon was wincing as his dad pulled his head to one side. Suddenly he let go and Devon stumbled. Regaining his balance, he ran to pull the bikes out of the way. His dad gunned the motor and the truck lurched forward a couple of feet and Devon, startled, fell backwards over Taylor's bike.

"God, you're clumsy," his dad yelled, laughing and shaking his head while Devon scrambled up and pulled the bikes aside. Taylor slipped back into the kitchen and Devon found her there, sitting at the counter as if she'd never moved.

"I wish I could come see you, Dev, I really, really do. I just can't."

"Then I'm coming to you," Devon said. "I'll find a way."

Taylor's heart sank. She'd been starting to think maybe she was safe here. Plus Gram and Douglas would be mad. She'd have to come right home after school every day in case Devon showed up. She couldn't risk him arriving and not finding her. He'd work himself into a terrible rage. He already accused her of cheating on him. The only silver lining was that if he came, he'd blow off some steam.

"Dev." Her voice was urgent. "You can't stay here if you come. Douglas would never let you." There was nowhere they could be private. She'd have to think of somewhere if he showed up. That was the best way for him to get relaxed.

The only other way was for him to beat her. The couple of times he had really pounded her, he was super nice afterward, for two or three weeks.

"Not if."

"When," she corrected herself hastily. "When. When are you coming?"

"I'll surprise you," Devon said. The little boy's voice was gone and a hard edge had replaced it.

"I love you," she whispered.

"You better," he said with a short laugh.

||||||

For a couple of weeks Taylor stuck close to home, picking Mason up or, if he was at Trevor's, doing her homework at the kitchen table while Douglas napped or watched television in the living room. Saturday mornings, when Taylor knew Devon wouldn't be out of bed until noon, she met Lily at the library. When they got bored with homework they played Hangman, or went to get coffee.

Lily had started passing Taylor the occasional evening babysitting job when she was too busy. Taylor would arrange for Mason to sleep over at Trevor's. She decided she would use the babysitting money, which mostly went for smokes, to get Lily something for Christmas. She could smoke less if she tried. There was a pair of earrings at the drugstore that would look perfect on Lily. They weren't too fussy. Just two long silvery chains hanging on either side. She'd seen Lily looking at them.

Taylor spoke to Devon on the phone twice but he never again mentioned coming, and Taylor was afraid to say anything in case he could tell she was worried about it. He might have just said it to scare her. Or he might be having trouble getting money for the bus. His father wouldn't let him drive his pickup, but his mom might let him use her old car if she didn't have to work for a couple of days.

Or he might just be biding his time. Devon had his own reasons for doing things.

Then he didn't call for a while, and Taylor started to relax.

Mason, who had always been a little slow, seemed to be catching up with the other kindergarteners. He still cried in his sleep now and then, but he'd stopped asking about Tannis. Taylor still had bad dreams sometimes, too, but she didn't see Tannis's face dripping blood anymore. She no longer woke up with her heart racing after dreaming about sitting in the passenger seat as her mother drove straight at an oncoming truck or a concrete barrier. Once she even dreamed she was able to grab the wheel and steer them onto the shoulder, where Virginia brought the car to a crunching halt, then turned to Taylor and gave her a hug. Taylor woke up from that one crying.

Eventually Taylor let herself slip back into spending some afternoons with Lily. They went to the library or hung out in Jay's basement, smoking a joint and eating Doritos.

About a week before Christmas, she and Lily walked to the Coke machine at lunch. Lily had drawn tiny faces on two fingertips of each hand and was holding them near Taylor's ear, using funny voices to issue running commentary on the people walking past them in the hall. She was funny without being mean — or anyway, without being too mean — and Taylor was grinning.

"Oh, Taylor, gonna have your addictive drink?" said right forefinger in a high squeaky voice as Taylor pushed her coins into the slot. "Always taking drugs, these young people," commented left forefinger in a fake baritone. "Just say no!" squeaked righty.

Taylor laughed as she dropped the can into her bag.

"Shut up," she said, elbowing Lily.

"Shut up, shut up," Lily mimicked in the several voices of her characters, waggling the fingertips in Taylor's face.

Taylor grabbed Lily's outstretched hands and held them away from her, palm to palm, feeling Lily push back, her height giving her a slight advantage, making Taylor almost lose her balance as she stumbled back against the vending machine.

For a second, Lily was pressed against her, and Taylor could smell her sweet hair and the warmth of her body. Immediately Lily sprang back and both girls dropped their hands. There was a moment of stillness, and then they both turned and headed for the caf.

They sat at the end of an empty table. Taylor noticed the marker smudges on Lily's bread as she held her bologna-on-white with her finger faces.

Taylor swallowed a bite of turkey sandwich.

"So what do you usually do for Christmas?" She was almost afraid to ask, because holidays were frequently baggage minefields. But she really wanted to know.

Lily shrugged. "My dad and my stepmom used to come to town. My dad still visits my uncles and my nana. He really liked to have these big family dinners, with, like, everybody there." Lily bit and chewed. "Grownups' table, kids' table." She put her half-eaten sandwich on top of its Baggie and began to peel the crust off the sides. "They'd come over in the afternoon and start in on my dad's eggnog. He'd always be standing by the bowl, drinking and trying to get everyone else to drink more. The kids all smoked up in the garage. They thought we didn't know they were sloshed."

Lily looked down at her picked-apart sandwich.

"Anyway, for the last few years it's just been me and my mom. My mom and dad don't want to see each other and I can't really leave my mom alone on the holiday."

Taylor pushed the last piece of her sandwich into her mouth and crumpled her bag.

"I don't know what to do for Mason," she said. This conversation was suddenly making her feel deeply tired. Lily knew the bare outlines of her life — her mom dying, then Tannis, and Devon being scary sometimes. But there was still too much to explain for anything to make sense.

"What do you usually do?" Lily asked, chewing the shreds of her crust.

"Well, my sister used to be alive. And before that, my mom."

If she could have any Christmas she wanted, thought Taylor, she'd send Gram and Douglas away with Mason. Then, in the quiet house, she'd have Lily over. They could cook mac and cheese, make chocolate chip cookies, watch old movies. Then they could fall asleep right there in a nest of pillows pulled off the couch and piled on the carpet in front of the TV, not needing to move for anything — tidy up, brush their teeth — anything.

"Sorry, T," Lily said. She put her hand over Taylor's for just a second, tapping Taylor's knuckles with the two smushy-faced fingers.

Taylor was gathering herself to reply when Lily lifted her right forefinger and waved the little face at Taylor.

"Sorry, T-Bone," she said in the high squeaky voice.

Taylor grinned and lightly punched Lily in the middle of her open palm.

"Shut up," she said.

Lily turned her finger to face herself.

"Shut up, Lily-liver," she said in a funny voice, smiling.

| | | | |

The last day of school before Christmas was pretty much a waste as far as work was concerned. In geometry they got their last quizzes back and went over them. Then the teacher handed out candy canes and had them spend a half hour doing math games that were actually almost fun.

In English, Mr. Trent played Christmas music on his

iPod while they wrote Christmas stories. Taylor set hers in heaven, and made Tannis a floaty angel who leaned over the edge of a cloud and dropped little presents down to earth. For a few minutes Taylor had to close her eyes and breathe slowly, but that passed.

In biology the desks all had little plastic tubs from the Dollar Store on them, filled with red and green foil-wrapped chocolate kisses. Mr. Assouad encouraged everyone to munch candy while he handed out their last test along with prizes — big stick-on ribbon bows with homemade labels for each student. Some were serious, like Top All-Around Grade for the Semester and Best Lab Grade. Some were goofy, like Most Creative Use of a Dissected Frog Foot. Lily won Most Impressive Scarf, at which she jumped up, grinning, and began to pull her scarf off. Taylor watched the stripes unwind — purple, lavender, pink, green — a new color every time Lily drew another length from her neck. Then Lily ran up to the front and draped the scarf from a couple of chart hooks at the top of the blackboard so it looked like a wacky but festive garland, prancing back with her big purple bow stuck on top of her head. It matched the thin purple fringe of her bangs perfectly.

Taylor was expecting a joke prize, too, so she was shocked when Mr. Assouad announced her prize as Most Dramatic Improvement. She went to the front of the room to collect her big blue bow and Mr. Assouad beamed at her, shaking her hand and then patting her back as she turned.

"Excellent job, Taylor," he said. "I look forward to working with you in future."

Taylor couldn't stop smiling, even when she got back to her seat and crammed her mouth with chocolate kisses.

After classes she turned to Lily on the spur of the moment and asked her to come to the park with her and Mason to make snow angels. It had finally snowed properly the night before, and the light, crisp powder was still on the ground.

They were outside, blowing smoke into the cold sunshine, walking toward the bus stop. Lily pretended to think it over, laid her forefinger against her lips, gazed up at the pale sky, cocked her head.

Then she broke into a grin. She tossed her cigarette butt into the gutter, pulled on her mitten and threw an arm loosely around Taylor's shoulders.

"What the heck," she said. "I'm angelic, right?"

Taylor elbowed her lightly in the side.

"Yeah, right," she said. They stopped to get Mason from the mom who kept him after kindergarten and then went to McDonald's to get a treat of fries. Mason skipped along holding Lily's hand, swinging her arm jerkily as he pulled ahead and then skipped back again. Taylor picked up his other hand and felt she was connected to Lily this way, like electricity.

The park was small, just an odd lot of land between two buildings. There was a war memorial at one end and a few bushes and benches, but mostly it was just snow broken by the tracks of a few dog walks.

Mason took off like an arrow, running and hooting, his feet tossing up little sprays of snow powder. Lily ran after him and tackled him, rolling over so he fell across her chest. She let him throw handfuls of snow in her face before she pretended to tickle him through his coat, making him howl, half-laughing, even though he couldn't possibly feel it.

They played until it was dark. Snow clotted around the cuffs of their jeans and the collars of their coats. Mason's face was pink, and the back of his head was snowy from making angels.

Finally they stood and, breathing steam into the air, shouldered their school bags for the trudge out of the park.

Lily had recently bought a cellphone with her babysitting money, and Taylor called home. It made her very happy when Gram said she could invite Lily for supper. Gram had bought a pizza kit. Mason loved making pizza, and Gram pointed out that there wouldn't be that much to clean up. Gram always had a reason like that for doing something nice, but Taylor knew it was her way of giving them an end-of-school treat. Taylor also knew Gram and Douglas would be pleased with her biology prize, although they might not say so.

Mason was stumbling along, clumsy from tiredness, although he perked up when Taylor told him it would be a pizza night. She invited Lily and held her breath for a couple of seconds until Lily said, "Okay. Thanks." Taylor could see that she was happy, and that made Taylor happy, too.

Mason shuffled loosely through the snow, falling behind. At the corner before their house, he sank to his knees and asked to be carried.

"Oh, my God," Lily cried, opening her arms wide. "You're way too big a boy to be carried!"

At that, Mason lay down completely. Taylor nudged him with her foot.

"Come on, Mace." He didn't move except to shake his head, his snowsuit hood making a swish-swish sound against the ground.

"Ma-ace," she said. He reached out and held her ankle with his small mittened hand. Taylor rolled her eyes, handed her bag to Lily and bent to pick him up. He lay against her chest like a sack of potatoes, his face bobbing gently against her shoulder as she walked.

He was heavy, but it was only half a block.

Christmas lights brightened the eaves and bushes in the front yards of the houses they passed. Taylor imagined a different supper being cooked in each home. Beef stew in the blue house with the snowman in front. Spaghetti and garlic bread in the white house with the green curtains. Roasted chicken with mashed potatoes in the house that had multi-colored Christmas lights blinking on their pine tree.

Taylor was resting her own head against the side of Mason's hood when she noticed a car parked behind Gram's in the driveway. She didn't recognize it. She said, "Here it is, Lily-liver," pointing to the front door with her chin, when someone moved out from behind the car and stood by the hood.

It took Taylor about a year to realize it was Devon.

"Who's this?" he called out, staring straight at Taylor but obviously referring to Lily.

"Dev," Taylor breathed. She was trying to keep fear out of her voice, calculating what mix of emotions she should let him hear even as his name escaped her lips.

Devon smiled a big rigid smile and stepped forward, opening his arms.

"Taylor. Aren't you glad to see me?" She could hear the hurt in his voice. He could disguise the fury but not the pain.

Taylor involuntarily stepped back, holding Mason

tighter against her chest, then immediately stepped forward again. She regretted that step back.

"Devon!" she called brightly, smiling and nodding between him and Lily. Lily was relaxed but alert, watching.

Now Taylor really wondered what kind of problems Lily's baggage had equipped her for.

"Devon, this is my friend from school, Lily. Lily, this is my boyfriend from home, Devon." She forced herself to step forward.

Instead of kissing her, Devon reached out and patted Mason's head.

"Hey, Macey boy, how are ya?" Mason turned his head inside his hood but the hood didn't move, so Mason only had one eye trained on Devon. "Put the kid down, Tay. Don't you think he's a bit big for being carried?"

Taylor put Mason down and gave him a gentle push to go stand with Lily. Devon immediately stepped forward and held Taylor's head as he gave her a long, soft kiss.

She started to relax. Maybe this wouldn't be so bad. He did love her, really was just lonely. He pulled his mouth away from hers. Gazing into her eyes, he slipped one hand into the collar of her coat and, under her scarf, twisted a thick pinch of flesh at the back of her neck, hard, and held it there, reapplying his mouth to hers and kissing her again, gently.

He finished kissing her and let go of her neck, hooking his arm around her shoulders.

Her neck burned where he'd pinched it.

"Go ahead inside," Taylor said to Lily, waving in the direction of the front door. For a split second she felt she was Tannis waving everyone away before a beating. But maybe if Lily and Mason went in without her, Gram would come out or, even better, send Douglas.

Lily took Mason's hand and turned toward the door.

"Hey, wait," Devon called loudly. Still gripping Taylor by the shoulders, he gestured to Lily to come back. "I should chat with my girl's new best friend, shouldn't I?"

Lily dropped Mason's hand and calmly dug her cigarettes and lighter out of her pocket. She lit one for herself and then held the pack out to Devon.

Nice, Taylor thought. Devon drew out a smoke and Lily lit it for him, then offered one to Taylor. Taylor shucked off a glove and took a cigarette, too. Next to Lily, Mason sat down on the sidewalk.

"So you're friends with my girl," Devon said, blowing smoke at his feet.

Lily smiled. "We're in the same biology class. We study together."

Devon nodded, drawing on his smoke.

Lily gestured with her chin. "Nice car. Yours?"

Devon gave a lopsided grin.

"I borrowed 'er," he said. He shrugged again, glancing back at the car, something red. A couple of dings in its side were touched up with an almost-matching color.

"Dev, you didn't take that car out of your dad's shop, did you?" Taylor's eyes were wide.

"None of your fucking business," Devon said. He turned and looked again. Following his glance, Taylor suddenly realized someone was sitting in the driver's seat.

"Who's that?" she asked.

Devon gave her shoulder a couple of quick squeezes, meaning he didn't like her asking.

"Oh, that. That's a friend of mine who drove out with me."

Taylor drew hard on her cigarette, filled her bloodstream with as much of the bracing cocktail of chemicals as she could. The silhouette in the car didn't move. Taylor had the sense that the person was watching them.

Lily stood, one arm across her stomach, the other bent, her cigarette held close to her mouth. She drew on it and then blew the smoke out in a slow, arrow-straight stream.

At Lily's feet, Mason lay on his back, his eyes like tiny pools of dark water in the darkness.

Devon turned to Lily. "You should take the kid inside." His voice was almost pleasant.

Without taking her gaze off Devon's face, Lily smiled. Then she looked down at Mason.

"Get up, Mace," she said in a commanding voice. Mason rolled over in his fat snowsuit and pushed himself up onto his knees, then stood. He grabbed onto Lily's coat pocket and the two of them turned and walked up to the front door. Lily knocked, leaning casually against the doorjamb and looking back around as she waited.

A moment later the door opened and Gram was there, dark against the light behind her. She looked out — at Lily, then Taylor, then Devon and the car. Mason stepped forward and clomped past her into the house.

"Devon," she said.

"Hi, Mrs. Linder."

"If I'd known you were coming I'd have gotten another pizza." Gram sounded mad, as if Taylor had known Devon was coming but hadn't said so.

"No problem," Devon said, waving the hand that wasn't gripping Taylor's shoulder.

Gram was silent for a moment, looking at them. Then she pulled her sweater closer around her and stepped back into the house.

"You kids come inside," she said and disappeared behind the closing door.

"Come inside, Dev." Taylor swung around and pressed against him, leaning her head to one side. "You can have my pizza. I'm not hungry. You can bring your friend."

Lily had detached herself from the doorframe and walked deliberately back to the sidewalk. She took a last drag on her smoke and threw it into the slush at the curb, then shoved her hands into her pockets.

"Yeah," she said. "Your friend can have mine. I'm not that big on pizza." Taylor marveled at how solidly Lily stood on the snow-covered concrete.

Devon paused, then turned to Taylor.

"Come for a ride," he said.

"I have to go in," Taylor answered, gesturing toward the house. "Come in."

"Come for a ride, Tay," Devon said again. Before she could stop herself, Taylor turned and glanced at Lily. Out of the corner of her eye she saw Devon see them looking at each other.

Devon stepped between the two girls, standing right in front of Taylor, his face directly in front of hers. He smiled and shook his head, as if amused, then lifted his gaze and looked into Taylor's eyes.

"Say goodnight to your friend and come for a ride with your loving boyfriend, Taylor." He put a hand on her waist and began to walk her sideways toward the car. The person in the driver's seat leaned over and opened the back passenger door.

Taylor felt frozen. She wished Gram would choose this moment to come out and see what was taking them so long, or send Douglas to give them a piece of his mind, but no one appeared.

As Devon, still gazing directly into Taylor's eyes, walked her toward the car, Taylor used all her mental strength to raise her arm and wave in Lily's direction.

"Lily ..." she began. Devon maneuvered her to the back door of the car and then put his hand on top of her head as she folded herself in, and for a moment she wondered where he'd learned that, whether it was from watching TV or whether he'd been in trouble with the police lately. Her blood felt full of bubbles, half panic and half hopelessness. She briefly wondered when she'd see Mason again. She hoped Gram would make the pizza kit with him.

Devon pushed Taylor across the back seat and got in with her, slamming the door.

The inside of the car was dark and smelled like cold air and cigarettes. The guy in the front seat gunned the engine.

And then the front passenger door opened, and just as the car peeled out of the driveway, Taylor saw Lily land in the front seat and pull the door closed, the front of the house already in motion through the windshield.

Devon's mouth dropped open. Lily turned around in the front seat and smiled.

"Where we going?" she asked.

Taylor thought she might just collapse with relief, and then one second later she was half panicked again. She didn't want anything to happen to Lily. But she was so glad to see Lily's tall, beautiful, solid form in the front seat. She groped for the seatbelt behind her as the car slid a little around a corner. She was afraid to look at Devon but she forced herself.

He was staring at Lily, and his expression was unreadable.

"I thought for a minute there you guys were gonna leave without me!" Lily cried cheerfully.

No one said anything. Taylor had never seen Devon at a loss for words, except with his father.

Lily turned again and sat facing front.

"Nice car," she said. "Mind if I turn up the heat a little?" And without waiting for an answer she reached over and turned the knob.

They drove in silence. Houses disappeared away into the darkness at the roadside as they sped past.

Taylor kept her eyes down, watching Devon's wide hand that enclosed both of hers in her lap. His left arm was draped heavily over her shoulder and he was sitting right up against her. The press of his big body didn't stop the subtle trembling that was exhausting her. They both watched as his hand squeezed her fingers, then opened; squeezed, then opened. At first she thought he was going to break her fingers, but he didn't. He squeezed hard but not too hard, the movement of his hand like a big skin heart.

"I'm gonna be in trouble with Gram," Taylor whispered.

"Don't talk to me about that slut bitch," Devon said, his voice deadly calm.

They were out on the highway now. In the dark Taylor didn't recognize the landscape. The wind blew long feathery streams of snow across the road and against the windshield. She felt the back end of the car fishtail occasionally as they sped past fields and black, broken skeletons of trees.

In the front seat, Lily lit a cigarette and passed it to the guy who was driving. He waited a beat and then took it.

"What's your name again?" she asked.

"Conor," he replied, almost under his breath.

Taylor felt guilty that Lily was here with them. Now that school was over, maybe no one would even look for them for ages.

That was stupid. Gram knew they'd driven away with Devon. She wouldn't just let Taylor disappear. But Gram didn't know how much he could hurt Taylor in the time it would take to find them. No one knew.

Taylor imagined Gram sitting at the kitchen table smoking while Mason, a dish towel tied around his neck, slopped tomato sauce onto the raw pizza dough. The thought reminded her that she was hungry, and tired the way she got when she was low on fuel.

"Dev," she whispered close to his ear. "Aren't you hungry?" She laid her head tiredly against his shoulder.

He didn't answer, but rummaged in the pocket of his jacket, pulling out a cigarette and lighting it. He took a couple of slow drags and then held it in front of Taylor's mouth, lifting his shoulder just slightly to get her attention.

That seemed like a good sign. She dragged on it and blew out. She closed her eyes and listened to the loud white sound of the car's wheels on the road, its engine and the closer sound of Devon breathing smoke in and blowing it out.

Then he sat up and cranked open the window to throw out his butt, letting in the roar of wind and a shock of cold.

"Go there, man," he said to Conor. Taylor lifted her head to look.

They were heading off the road. There was a garish stain of neon ahead. Devon pushed Taylor's head back down against his shoulder, his open palm passing down over her face to close her eyes, as if she were a corpse. She breathed as quietly as she could until her blood slowed to normal.

Six

WHEN LILY'S FATHER told the story of her mother's brain injury, he made it sound as if — during the months her mother was in hospital — he and Lily were happy companions, just the two of them. He described tucking her in at night, going to the playground after supper, going to movies on weekends.

Mostly Lily remembered staying at Nana's, though she did remember going to a movie with him. She had a pack of red licorice in her lap. It lay heavy across her thighs, the plastic wrapper crinkling loudly when she tried to tear it open. Her father nipped from his flask after the lights went down.

She remembered staying at Nana's house a lot. She was put to bed on the couch in Nana's sewing room, and she was afraid of having one of those dreams of flooding warmth that ended with waking up and finding herself tangled in cold wet sheets. She was frustrated by how difficult her own body was to control — how when it got urgent she was powerless to stop herself peeing, or how her fingers were thick and stupid when she tried to tie her shoes.

She didn't think she ever did pee the couch at Nana's. She didn't have any memory of confusion, shame, Nana frowning down at her.

What she did remember was Uncle Gil coming home late from his job at the restaurant or after going dancing with his friends, and sneaking in to wake her up.

"Come on, girlfriend," he'd whisper in her ear as he scooped her out of bed. They would tiptoe downstairs in the quiet house, and he would sit her on a phone book at the kitchen table so she could eat a bowl of ice cream with him. Uncle Gil always picked a handful of peanuts out of the blue can of mixed nuts with the yellow plastic lid and crushed them by rolling a can of soup over them. Then he sprinkled them on their ice cream.

Lily loved Uncle Gil with all her heart. When high school was lonely, or dead boring, she imagined leaving — maybe even the day after graduation — and going to visit him in California, where he was working in another restaurant. Sometimes, instead of cheese popcorn, she bought herself salted peanuts. After eating them she smelled her fingers, and it made her think of him.

She thought of him now. They'd pulled into a rest stop, and Lily could just about make out the poster in the restaurant window featuring a Peanut Parfait. The tall glass appeared to be filled with vanilla and chocolate swirled together, a fat cluster of crushed peanuts carpeting the top.

Water came into her mouth. She hadn't eaten since lunch, and then only part of a sandwich. She hoped Devon would let them eat now.

There was silence in the car, the engine ticking. Light flakes of snow drifted past the windshield. Passing headlights made Conor's head glow briefly.

Uncle Gil had bright, shiny blond hair that Lily was surprised one day to find him bleaching in the bathroom. "A girl's gotta keep up appearances," he'd said, winking.

Moving only her eyes, she glanced at the side mirror. She didn't know what they were waiting for. The car was getting cold. She couldn't see Taylor's face, only the corner of her shoulder. Their breath was coming out in thin clouds. Lily's mitts and coat collar were damp from their snow play and it was making her cold, and irritating the skin on the back of her neck. She wanted to rewind her long scarf so it was inside her coat collar, but she didn't want to move until she could judge Devon's mood.

Finally she took out her cigarettes.

"Want?" she asked Conor, holding the pack out without looking at him. He looked down and slid out a cigarette.

Lily took one herself and held her lighter out for Conor. She lit her own cigarette and then, as if she had just remembered that Devon and Taylor were in the back seat, turned and held out the pack again.

Taylor's head was on Devon's shoulder and her eyes were closed, but her face didn't have the softness of someone sleeping.

Devon took a cigarette and nudged the box back at Lily.

"We'll share," he said. Lily reached over and struck her lighter for him. It flared up in the darkness. He stuck the cigarette into his mouth and leaned forward. In the light of the flame Lily saw his square head, like a boxer's. He pulled on the smoke until it glowed red, then sat back again, read-justing his arm around Taylor's shoulder. He was so much bulkier than Taylor, they almost seemed like two different kinds of animals.

Lily considered proposing that she go inside to buy more cigarettes, but she didn't want them to drive away without her. She cracked her window and aimed her smoke at the crack, watching it turn whiter as it fed out into the night, feeling cold air slip in past her face.

She was startled when Conor spoke.

"Coffee?" he said.

"Yeah," Devon said. "Sounds good." He sounded agree-able, even enthusiastic. Lily heard them shifting around in the back seat. "Hey, sit up, you stupid bitch," Devon said with a short laugh.

"Dev," Taylor said softly. Lily could imagine her looking at Devon, moving her eyes in the direction of the front seat, then looking back.

"Don't tell me what to do," Devon said, but his tone was still friendly. She turned to see him hook his arm around Taylor's head and pull it close, press his lips to her forehead. Devon took a long drag, opened the car door and tossed his butt. Lily saw it land on the thin layer of clean snow that lay on top of the dirty, half-frozen slush. The coal winked as it sank into the wet and went out.

"Let's go," Devon said.

Lily wished she knew how to read Devon. Her mother had a boyfriend once who was mean leading up to a fight, then totally friendly after the storm of violence had passed. Another one would be in a good mood, pouring out drinks, telling Lily's mom how beautiful her hair was, fantasizing about going somewhere warm over the holidays. Lily's mom would start to glow.

"Then again," he'd say, turning slowly and reaching out and taking a fistful of Lily's mom's hair. He'd be smiling, and Lily's mom would be smiling, and Lily's skin would be crawling, and she'd jump when he suddenly stood up and roared, "I wouldn't want to go anywhere with such an ugly bitch!" And that would be the beginning of a beating.

They all piled out of the car, Lily lifting herself out of the front seat slowly so she could be sure they were all really going into the restaurant. The press of danger, which had kept her strung tight, was starting to make her tired. She concentrated, refocused herself like the lens of a camera, sharp again.

Conor walked around the front of the car and set off alone, not looking back. Lily walked just behind Taylor. Devon had his arm draped loosely across Taylor's shoulders, and she had her arm tight around his waist, her fist clutching the side of his jacket, her head snuggled against his shoulder.

Lily watched Conor disappear inside the restaurant. A family spilled out of the double glass doors, light and noise and the smell of fried food spilling out with them. Devon, Taylor and Lily waited for them to pass, and then they all walked in together. There was music playing, and the sound of voices, and some kind of machine — someone making a milkshake, maybe.

Then she saw the sign and grabbed Taylor's hand.

"Let's go pee," she said brightly. Taylor looked at Devon. He looked at her from under his dark brows and let his arm slip off her shoulders.

God, Lily thought, she even needs permission to pee. Her mother got slapped around sometimes, but even retarded as she was, she never asked her stupid boyfriends if she could pee.

Lily slid her arm around Taylor's shoulder where Devon's had been.

"C'mon, girlfriend," she said.

"Meet ya inside," Devon said, turning toward the rows of booths, his hands shoved inside the pockets of the hoodie he was wearing under his winter jacket. His elbows jutted out to the sides.

In the bathroom, the fluorescent light hit Lily flat in the face. She could see Taylor's feet in the next stall. Her thin boots looked damp. Lily heard Taylor's pee burble against the inside of the toilet bowl. Only then did she realize she hadn't yet let go of her own.

At the sinks, Lily looked down at her soapy hands and said, "Where we going?"

"I don't know."

"What do you want to do?"

Taylor shrugged, and then took a quick breath. "I don't know. He's never done this before. I thought he was going to take us to his place, but I don't know where we are." Her voice was thin and quavery. She bent over the running water and splashed her face. Her hair slid forward and Lily saw that there were dark red bruises on the back of her neck.

"I have my cell," Lily said. "Should we call someone?"

"I can't," Taylor said. "He'll be really mad."

"We can call the police."

"No. I don't want him to get in trouble. Besides, if I did that, he'd come back after me. Please don't," she whispered urgently.

Lily looked around the bathroom. She knew Taylor would say that. She put her hand in her coat pocket and fingered the phone.

"My gram's going to be really mad," Taylor said, her voice strained. "It's too much extra work for her to take care of Mason."

Lily held out the phone. "Just call your gram and tell her where we are so she won't worry."

"No, I can't. She'll tell me to come home and then when I don't she'll be even more furious. She's gonna be so disappointed in me. She doesn't understand what it's like."

Lily shook her head. "We'll get back as soon as we can. You can try to explain when we're home."

Taylor's voice was on the edge of breaking. "No," she cried. "She'll say why did you get in the car with him."

Good question, Lily wanted to say. But she knew it would just stress Taylor out more.

"We'll deal with that when we get back."

When they got to the booth, the boys slid out and let the girls take the inside seats. There were bright glossy menus on the table.

Conor, Devon and Lily ordered burgers and fries and coffees. When it was Taylor's turn, she shook her head.

"I'm not hungry," she said apologetically to the waitress.

Lily leaned forward. "You have to eat." She was startled to hear her own voice come out so stern. "How about soup? That's easy." Lily turned to the waitress and smiled. "What's your soup?"

"Chicken noodle or beef barley."

"Oh, man, I hate barley!" Devon said. "Barley's fucking disgusting. All those little slimy balls in your mouth."

Taylor made a little face at Lily, who gave her a tiny wink. Taylor looked up at the waitress.

"I'll have a chicken noodle, please, and extra crackers."

The waitress swept up the menus and turned away.

"Extra crackers," Lily repeated. "My mom's extra crackers." Taylor gave a wry grin. Devon and Conor looked blank.

Conor had pulled the little wire sugar-packet holder into the middle of the table and was making a pile of the sugar packets, trying to get them all in a stack before they fell over. Devon was watching his own fingers tap the Formica tabletop.

"So," Lily said, "where we going?"

There was a long silence.

"Little trip," Devon said.

"Yeah, obviously," Lily said, keeping her voice happy. "But where?"

"It's a surprise," Devon said. Lily thought he didn't even know himself, but then Conor flashed him a glance, and she decided that they did have a destination, and Conor knew what it was.

She looked over at Conor's sugar stack. With a single quick movement, she slipped a blue Equal packet out of the wire holder and stuck it in Conor's pile just as he was adding another sugar.

He looked up at her and she looked right back at him. She saw that he had clear light brown eyes and a tiny thread-like scar above one of his eyebrows. She wondered why he was here.

He looked down at his pile and hesitated. Lily thought he would take off the top sugar packet and flick away her blue one, but instead he added another sugar on top.

Lily's shoulders relaxed a little. She hadn't even known they were so tense.

The food came. Lily was starving and ate her burger in minutes. It tasted really good, and she felt strength flow into her as the food went down. Taylor closed her eyes with each spoonful, as if to stop herself from even seeing the soup, but she ate most of it. Lily bought a pack of cigs when she paid her bill. She could go for a long time without food now, but she'd hate to be short of smokes.

They piled back into the car, Devon and Taylor in the back seat again. Lily hunched against the cold and watched their hot damp breath steam the windshield white. When it started to clear she saw the Peanut Parfait poster again, and wished she'd thought of getting one.

They pulled out of the parking lot and drove into darkness, headlights flashing past them here and there, their own headlights washing across a green highway sign from time to time. The place names seemed vaguely familiar to Lily, but not enough to tell her where they were going. All she knew was that it was dark on all sides, with the dull light of snow when they passed a field, the dark shapes of bare trees and the black walls of evergreens lining the sides of the road.

As the car got warmer, Lily felt her eyelids get heavier. She wished she had another coffee, a big one with a lot of cream and sugar to hold between her bare hands. She wondered if they'd pass some place where they could drive through.

She was determined not to fall asleep, not to let her guard down.

And then the car turned and began to drive along a

crunchy road, and it woke her up. She had a moment of panic. They were in darkness, the sky slightly lighter above them, a wall of trees blocking their view on either side.

Where the hell were they?

She heard Devon give one of those groans that people make in the morning when they stretch their arms, and a muffled exchange between him and Taylor, and she figured they'd fallen asleep, too.

She shook her head. It was amazing how exhausting adrenaline could be. She remembered her mother falling asleep after one of the mean boyfriends threatened to cut her throat with a knife. It was more difficult than he expected, apparently, and she'd pushed his hand away. He threw down the knife in disgust and left the house. To Lily's astonishment, her mother slumped onto the couch, had a cry and then promptly nodded off.

Lily glanced over at Conor. He looked relaxed but alert. Perhaps he wasn't on the high wire with the rest of them.

"Almost there," Devon said.

Just then the moon broke through an opening in the trees and shone silver into the car. Ahead, a squat building was barely visible in the shadow of the tall trees behind it.

The car pulled up.

They all got out and stretched their legs, the girls hugging themselves against the icy air.

"My dad's cottage," Devon said. He went to the side of the house and rummaged in the shadows next to a woodpile, returning with an ax.

Lily stiffened. Devon walked casually over to the front door of the cabin and, with a grunt, struck one hard blow with the butt of the handle. He kicked the broken padlock to the side and pushed the door open. Lily willed him to put the ax back before going inside, and he did.

She tried to take Taylor's hand. Taylor squeezed very briefly and then slipped her hand out of Lily's, not looking at her.

Inside, a damp, musty smell like old cardboard and dust was sharp in her nose. Devon turned on a big square flashlight that sat on a table near the door. In its beam he fumbled with something else on the table. Lily heard him strike a match and the room leapt into existence. Devon turned a key on the side of a lantern and the flame shot up inside the glass chimney. They all turned their heads from the brightness for a moment until he figured out how to adjust the light.

Lily squinted as her eyes adjusted.

It was a small room, with what appeared to be a single bedroom off to the left. There was nothing homey or cute about it. The interior walls were painted plywood. There was a gun rack on one wall, with one gun in it, and a padlocked cupboard next to that.

Devon lit a second kerosene lantern and, holding it up, walked around. He examined everything, sticking his head into the room off the side. He lit a third lantern and took it in there, leaving it to throw big dark shadows through the door as he returned to continue his tour of the main room. He peered into an old trunk by the bedroom door. He looked like an inspector of some kind, keeping a tally in his mind. He leaned into a doorway and then held up a bucket.

"For the middle of the night," he said, grinning. "Otherwise, outside."

Conor groaned.

In front of the small fireplace, Devon knelt and looked up into the chimney.

Lily shivered inside her coat and pulled her big scarf up to cover her mouth, huffing warm breath into it and holding it against her face.

"Hey, make a fire. It's freezing in here," she said.

"Don't tell me what to do, bitch."

Lily looked at Taylor and rolled her eyes with a little smile, but Taylor just looked away.

"I'll do it," Conor said.

"No. I don't want anyone to know we're here by the smoke."

"It's fucking freezing, and we're in the middle of fucking nowhere, man! Who's gonna see it? Who's gonna care, anyway?" Conor was hugging himself and stamping his feet.

"It's not that cold. Don't be a pussy," Devon said. He went over to the one old couch and tossed the cushions on the floor. They all stood and watched him. Then he opened the trunk and started to pull blankets out of it.

He threw a couple of blankets on the couch and nodded at Conor, who said, "No way, man." Devon stood and stared at him until Conor finally rolled his eyes, then shrugged. "Fuck," he muttered, shaking his head, stepping over to pick up a gray blanket. Devon took another armful of blankets and, with his free hand, steered Taylor to the door of the side room, then stopped. He was gripping Taylor's arm above the wrist.

He turned and looked at her, then Lily.

"Best Friend, you stay with Conor," he said. "Do what he says. And I'll tell you both, right fucking now..."

He paused, then walked over to the padlocked cupboard. Lily was invisibly tied to the sight of him. He was pulling a taut string between himself and each of them, and she hated it, but she couldn't take her eyes off him.

He picked up a poker from the fireplace and used it to try to break the padlock off, but it was too high up for him to get a good angle.

Finally, he raised the poker and gave an angry cry as he smashed the handle right off the cupboard, padlock still attached.

Inside the cupboard were dusty boxes. Devon quickly and smoothly lifted the gun off the rack and loaded it with shells, then turned and raised the gun toward the room. Lily stood rigid.

"Don't fuck with me," Devon said. Then he pushed Taylor ahead of him into the small bedroom.

|||||

The next morning Lily thought she'd woken up before anyone else, but when she turned over in her nest of blankets, Conor wasn't there. A moment later she smelled cigarette smoke and heard him exhale.

The night before, he settled himself on the bare springs of the couch with the gray blanket over him, leaving her the cushions on the floor. She lay down without taking her coat or boots off, and immediately felt her hip sink down between two cushions onto the icy floor. She lay there, straining against the dark to hear. She was steeling herself to run into Devon and Taylor's room, although she knew from living with her mother that it wasn't always easy to tell the difference between the sounds of violence and sex. She also knew that people didn't always want help when they were being hurt. You could make things worse.

Lying in the dark, Lily's stomach ached. She wondered whether Taylor's gram would be worried, or just mad. Her own mother didn't keep track of her comings and goings. She probably wouldn't think to check whether Lily was even home tonight.

One less thing to worry about.

She couldn't hear anything anyway, except the wind outside and the rattling of tree branches. Sometimes a big gust threw a plume of icy snow against the windows with a clatter. Lily's jaw began to stiffen from the freezing air, and she huddled further inside her coat. Then she heard Conor shifting around, and the creak of the couch springs.

"Fuck this," he said in a low voice. He stood up.

"Shove over," he said, pushing her with his boot, although not in a mean way. She felt a wave of cold air as her blanket was lifted away from her, and then Conor lay down right behind her on the cushions and arranged both blankets over the two of them. He threw his arm over her waist and pulled himself up against her, shrugging down beneath the blanket edges.

"Nothing personal," he muttered into her hair. "It's just fucking freezing."

Lily took a moment to adjust to the unfamiliar feeling of another body against hers. He was just her height. His breath was warm and moist against the back of her head. His narrow pelvis pressed against the back of her coat. His boots lay heavy against her feet.

She felt jealous of Taylor, who was at least warm in a bed, skin against skin with someone she loved.

Then Lily frowned. Given the choice, she would rather be cold on the floor with someone who didn't care about her but wouldn't hurt her. Some choice.

She lay awake for a while, listening to Conor's even breathing and the wind outside. Her body ached from cold and tiredness. She hated that Devon had that gun, she hated that she had let herself be tricked into being stuck in the middle of fucking nowhere. Well, she was the one who jumped into the car. But she couldn't let them drive away with Taylor. She hated that this was happening, all because Devon was a big asshole.

A tear quivered in the corner of each eye until finally one slipped across the bridge of her nose and down her cheek, leaving a cold track on her face. She wanted to pound the floor with her fist. Her skinny biceps flexed as she thought about it, until she slipped into sleep.

Now Lily pushed herself up, holding a blanket around her shoulders, and walked over to the frosty window. At first the glare of the light reflecting off the snow hurt her eyes. All she could see was snow and trees, and beyond the trees the thick darkness of forest. The roof of the car was thinly frosted, as if someone had blown a giant handful of sugar over it in the night.

Lily turned. Conor was sitting at the little table. His hand was slowly ashing his cigarette on the edge of the ashtray, but he was looking right at Lily.

"What," she said.

"You should make some coffee."

"Why, because I'm a girl?" She rolled her eyes.

"Yeah," he said. What an asshole. Fuck you very much, as Uncle Gil used to say. On the other hand, if she made coffee she could drink some.

She clumped over to the cupboards and began to open them. Cups and plates, an old-fashioned tin coffee pot. A salt shaker. She picked it up and shook it. Almost empty, but not quite. A scattering of little black nuggets, just like the ones on the counter.

Lily kept rummaging. There were a few pieces of cutlery in the drawers, a box of wooden matches, but that was it.

No coffee, no food, no supplies of any kind. Now that Conor had mentioned coffee, she was really craving it. She turned and leaned against the counter, arms crossed, and looked at him. He was ignoring her, watching his cigarette burn to the filter. She walked over and took a cigarette out of his open pack, stuck it in her mouth and lit it with his lighter. She saw his muscles tighten and then release. He was choosing not to argue with her.

Good to know.

She leaned back against the counter again and inhaled.

"There's no coffee," she said. "No fucking anything, in fact, except mouse turds."

Conor closed his eyes slowly and tipped his head back. She could see his lips moving, mouthing fuck, fuck, fuck. She wondered what Devon had told him to convince him to come along on this stupid trip. Probably not that they'd be freezing their asses in the woods without even a fucking coffee.

"Maybe we can make mouse turd coffee," Lily said. "Have some mouse eggs and mouse bacon, little mousey toast."

"Shut up," Conor said. "I'm gonna go get some coffee. Tell Devon when he comes out." Lily watched him zip his jacket to the neck as he walked to the door. "And pick that up," he said, gesturing toward the mess of blankets and cushions on the floor.

"Bring some breakfast," Lily called after him. "Asshole," she added as she took a short drag on her smoke.

After she replaced the couch cushions and folded the blankets, she lit one of her own cigs and sat down on the couch, knees up against her chest. She pulled her phone out of her coat pocket and saw that there was no reception. She wished she'd called someone from the restaurant. But what would she have said? We're being held prisoner by some friends of ours, whose car we got into in front of Taylor's own house? They let us go to the can by ourselves and we can make a phone call, but we're still prisoners?

She picked at some ragged skin around her thumbnail. She tried to bite off a piece of that loose skin, but it was too small. She couldn't find it with her teeth. She thought of her mother, the men she went out with. Maybe they even picked you because they knew you'd be easy to push around.

How did people know these things?

She finished her cig and just sat on the couch, wondering how long it would take Conor to get back with coffee. She'd been stupid to fall asleep in the car last night, because now she didn't know how long it had taken them to drive from the rest stop to the cabin.

There was no sound from behind the bedroom door. Where there was also a gun. Her heart trotted inside her chest. She wished Conor would come back, although she knew it was irrational to feel safer with him around.

She began to imagine all the things she wanted Conor to bring back for breakfast. An Egg McMuffin. A yogurt with fruit on the bottom and granola in the plastic cup on top. Or buttered toast wrapped in a paper napkin, with those little plastic peanut butters and a plastic knife to spread it with. Maybe he'd bring orange juice.

She lit another cigarette. It wasn't food, but it was better than nothing.

It occurred to her to wonder whether Conor would come back at all. If it was her, she wouldn't. She'd just go home, take a hot shower and make herself a big coffee with a heaping spoonful of her mother's Coffee-mate. She'd drink it while she made a pot of mac and cheese and eat that out of the pot in front of the TV.

She could see herself and Taylor sitting on the floor with their backs against the old plaid couch, eating frozen pizza, watching reruns. *Friends*, or *The Simpsons*. Homer reminded her of her mother a little bit, although he wasn't brain-injured, just stupid.

Outside, the wind seemed to have died down, and Lily realized she could hear something, a ratchety sound from the bedroom. It faded in and out. Then she heard the faint sound of a voice, and she suddenly understood that Devon and Taylor were having sex.

At first she felt embarrassed. Then she stood up. It meant that for sure they wouldn't come out for a little while.

She wound her big scarf around her neck, all the way up until it covered her chin, then tucked the ends into her coat. If she didn't have to be a prisoner, she wouldn't be.

The tiredness drained out of her limbs and was replaced by a feeling of strength. She pulled on her damp mittens and flipped up her hood and walked out into the weak sunshine, careful not to let the door bang shut behind her.

The snow was high, but if she didn't stomp too hard, the surface crust would mostly hold her. The times it didn't, her boot tops filled with snow and her jeans got wet, but it couldn't be helped.

She followed Conor's tire tracks, walking for ages under the dark tunnel of trees. She startled at the sounds of branches cracking in the cold.

Finally she emerged onto a road.

She had to look closely to figure out which way Conor had turned. She turned that way, keeping to tracks he'd made in the blown snow, watching for his approach in the distance.

Until Conor returned, Devon might assume Lily had gone with him. She kept an eye out for places to take cover on the side of the road.

After about half an hour of trudging, she passed a turnoff, but she couldn't see any tire tracks anymore, so she kept walking forward. She talked to herself in the voices of the faces she sometimes drew on her fingers.

"Keep it moving, Lily-liver," she said in a high voice, wiggling one finger inside her mitten.

Her breath started to come raw in her throat, but she kept walking. Except for the whine of the wind, all she could hear was the snow crunching and squeaking under her boots. Occasionally she saw the black shape of a lone bird overhead.

She was shocked when she heard an engine, and Conor appeared in the red car behind her. She stood and gaped at him. Her heart was pounding so hard she felt herself shaking.

He pulled up and jumped out of the car, walked over

and grabbed her by the back of her hood. He was pulling some of her hair, too, but it hardly mattered. He opened the passenger door and shoved her toward it. She stumbled and he pushed her again. She barely ducked her head in time to avoid hitting the car roof.

He slammed the door shut and strode over to get in on the driver's side. His face looked grim. He turned to her and grabbed her chin, squeezing it hard as he forced her to face him.

"Do not fuck with me," he said, his voice horribly calm and low. He was squeezing her face so hard she could feel his fingers digging into her gums. She didn't move, didn't even blink. "Ever," he said. "Again."

He slowly turned away.

Lily felt desperate. What if this was her last chance? She'd blown it at Taylor's and at the restaurant. If she let him take her back to the cabin it would be worse.

"Let me go," she blurted. "Just drop me off somewhere. Say you didn't see me." She could hear the pleading sound in her voice and hated it. She saw a muscle twitch in Conor's jaw, but he moved so fast she didn't see his big hand until it slammed her head back against the car window.

He was on his knees on the front seat, looming over her, his face so close to hers that she could see two tiny blackheads at the corner of his nose.

"Devon has a gun," he whispered, "but I can kill you with my bare hands."

Then, without looking at her, he sat back down and began to drive.

Seven

Taylor seesawed between hoping that Lily got away and being furious with her for making Devon mad. She was sure she was going to get a beating because Lily had made a break for it. She wouldn't cry, for her own sake and because it would irritate Devon. But at the same time she was filled with sadness and hope and love for Lily.

Lily was so brave.

Kneeling on the couch, Taylor methodically kneaded Devon's shoulders through his T-shirt, her hands under the collar of his open parka. She was also mad at Lily because she'd let Devon fuck her this morning even though they didn't have any condoms, to help him relax, because when he was this stressed was exactly when he was likely to go off on her.

She thought he would want to do it last night, but when he pushed her into the freezing little room he was lost in his own thoughts. They took their jackets and boots off and got under the rough covers in their clothes, their cold sock feet against each other's legs. He slipped his icy hands into her armpits and they shivered against each other. She waited, but he fell asleep, his breath warm against her face.

He woke her by pulling her jeans off under the covers. It took her a few moments to emerge from the foggy-headedness of sleep. She put her palms against his chest and looked him in the face.

"Dev," she whispered, "don't forget protection."

"Don't got any," he grunted, pushing her hands away, positioning himself.

"Dev, we said we wouldn't without protection — "

"Shut up, Tay."

He wouldn't bother to argue with her. She could try to physically fight him off, but even if she succeeded, he'd definitely beat the shit out of her. On the other hand, if she let him fuck her, he'd be relaxed for sure. So she decided to let him. To swap one kind of being safe for another.

After he came he lay on top of her and kissed her temples and played with her hair and told her he loved her and that she was so beautiful, and she'd been really glad she'd talked herself into doing it.

It was one of their best times ever, actually. He was calm and happy, and she started to relax, let his love for her soak in through her skin and make her full. Sometimes when he was really mean to her, or hit her, she told herself that he didn't really love her, because if he did he could never treat her this way. But this morning she'd felt sure, and hopeful.

Now that risk was wasted. Conor had come back with the coffee and found Lily gone, and Devon totally lost it.

He grabbed the gun and actually hit Conor on the shoulder with the long part of it, and she didn't know who was more scared, her or Conor.

Now, waiting for Conor to come back, Devon's shoulders and back were like concrete. She kneaded and kneaded and he groaned. She could feel his back loosening up just a little bit. Then she stuck her thumb in a tender spot by mistake. She knew it was wrong even as she was doing it, but she couldn't stop herself in time, and without even turning he rammed his elbow backwards into her stomach and she pitched over, feeling bile come up into her throat as she hit the floor.

She choked and sputtered and it took her several minutes to lift herself up and unbend her mid-section, which hurt so much she thought he'd ruptured something. When she finally sat up and wiped her hair out of her face, she saw that he was still sitting on the couch facing the door, watching for Conor and Lily.

Taylor's throat burned, and she was trying to decide whether she could go get some water when Devon said, "Get up here and finish what you started."

She climbed back up on the couch, swallowing hard. Devon was such an asshole! The way he spoke to her was just the way his father spoke to him. She felt sorry for him being treated that way, but that was no excuse to do it to other people.

She began to massage carefully. She hated it when he talked to her like that. Stroking the hard muscles along the sides of his neck, she let herself imagine being strong enough to close his windpipe, just like pinching a large straw.

They both heard the car pull up. Lily came through the

door first, stone-faced, not looking at anyone. She shuffled over to the little table and sat down.

That scared Taylor. She'd never seen Lily look so beaten. Then Lily seemed to come back to herself a little. Using one finger, she pulled the cardboard carrier toward her and detached a cup of coffee, pried the lid off and took a gulp. She made a face, then drank more.

Conor, still hunched in his jacket, sat down in the other chair and helped himself to one of the coffees.

They looked like two kids who had been fighting with their parents.

Lily had some kind of smudges on her face. It was hard to tell in the dull light. They almost looked like bruises, but they were only small, and in an odd place near her jaw.

Maybe she knocked into a branch while she was walking to the road.

"It's as fucking freezing in here as it is outside," Conor muttered.

"Go outside then," Devon replied.

Everyone sat, not speaking, their heads bent. Devon looked pleased with himself. Taylor felt his back and shoulders relax under her hands. She leaned forward and nuzzled his neck. He reached back and tenderly stroked her cheek. It almost made her love him in that moment.

Conor was eating a donut, cramming it into his mouth half at a time, chewing it in one big ball at the back of his jaw. Lily was peeking into the paper bags that were lying on the table. She crumpled an empty one, then drew a muffin out of another.

She was just starting to peel the paper off one side when Devon, moving unbelievably fast, darted off the couch and grabbed the muffin out of Lily's hand, squashing it as he held it up in front of her face, which Taylor was thrilled to see remained blank.

"You think I should let you eat, you traitor bitch?" he said quietly.

Taylor's breath stopped in her throat. She wished with all her heart that Lily hadn't gotten into the car with them. She began to hate Lily for making her feel responsible for her.

Lily just sat, not moving, her eyes dead.

"Please, Dev. Let her eat. She's not your girlfriend," she said. He turned around and she thought for a second that might have made him angrier, but his face relaxed. He smiled at her. His expression said, Silly Taylor. Then, still smiling, he opened his hand and let the crumbled muffin fall onto the table in front of Lily. He came back over and sat down in front of Taylor again, facing the little table, and motioned for her to continue rubbing his shoulders.

"You shouldn't interfere, Tay," he said, his voice light. She leaned in and put her chin on his shoulder.

"I'm sorry, baby," she whispered.

"You should know better," he said. There was a pause as he leaned back into his massage. "You showed very bad judgment in your choice of best friend. You're going to have to change that when we get back home."

"I will," she said. She was embarrassed. She usually wasn't this submissive in front of other people. It made her feel small in front of Lily.

But then, she thought, I am small. This is the way small people behave. Devon makes me make myself small. I let Devon make me make myself small...

She followed herself so far into that thought that she was trapped in the tiny end of it, and had to punch her way out. She felt the ache in her belly from Devon's elbow.

She took a breath.

"When are we going home, then?" she asked. The acid in her stomach sizzled.

A silence filled up the cabin as Taylor's words hung in the air. Both Conor and Lily turned to look.

Devon smiled at them.

"I'll decide," he said.

Conor stretched one of his long legs under the table and broke another donut in two.

"I have to work, man."

"Don't worry," Devon replied.

Taylor suddenly remembered that it would be Christmas in two days.

"It's Mason's first Christmas without my sister, Dev. Please, can't I be with him for that? I'll come back with you for as long as you want after." She heard the water in her voice and tried to firm it up as she spoke.

"We might spend Christmas here," Devon said. "We could get some decorations, some candles. There's nothing but trees out there!" He grinned, opening one arm in the direction of the door.

Taylor didn't say anything. If they were still here at Christmas, someone would start a search. Unless they all had fucked-up families.

She wondered whether Gram would ever call the police. She imagined Mason sitting in the dry bathtub at Gram's like he had at the hotel, playing with his blocks, missing her.

"Conor, man," Devon said. "Tie that bitch up." He lifted

his chin toward Lily. "Not, like, you know, completely. Just, like, her ankles or something, so she can't get away again."

Conor stared at Devon.

"What the fuck, man," Conor said quietly. "Let her go. She'll freeze to death before she gets within miles of anything." He pulled his smokes out of his jacket pocket and lit one.

"Tie her up," Devon repeated.

Conor didn't answer. Taylor concentrated on the muscles under Devon's shoulder blades, watching Lily's tense profile as she slowly ate her muffin crumb by crumb.

There was a long silence, and then Devon reached back and pushed Taylor's hands off him.

"Whatever," he said. He stood up. "You should eat something," he said to Taylor. "Have some delicious cold coffee."

Taylor's stomach still hurt where Devon had rammed his elbow into her, and she had no appetite at all. But she remembered Lily telling her to eat at the restaurant. She took a cup of coffee and a donut and sat on the edge of the couch. She sipped at the coffee and pinched off the sugared edges of the donut and stuffed them into her mouth, letting them dissolve there.

Devon found a rope in a cupboard. Lily jumped up as he approached, but he grabbed her shoulder and slammed her back into her chair. She was as tall as he was, but he was bulky and muscular.

He held Lily in her chair and said, "If you move again I'll shoot your face off."

Lily turned her face away, but sat still.

Taylor tried to think where Devon had left the gun. It was out here before, when Devon hit Conor with it, but she couldn't see it now.

Devon sat on the floor behind Lily's chair and improvised a complicated series of loops and knots around her ankles, with one end attached to the crossbar of the chair. Then he stood up and looked at Lily.

"How am I supposed to go pee?" Lily asked in a clear voice.

Taylor had a tiny moment of fear and glee. Lily was crazy brave. It made Taylor almost ill, thinking of how she'd sucked up to Devon earlier, kissing him and telling him she loved him, saying "Please, baby." All in that little-girl voice he liked.

"Pee your fucking pants," he said.

"If she pees her pants," Conor said, "I'm out of here. I'm not staying in a fucking refrigerated hut in the fucking woods that smells like fucking pee!"

Devon smiled. He turned to Lily. "When you have to pee, walk your chair out the door and pull down your pants and pee in the snow like a dog. And if you want to keep going," he added, "you can drag your fucking chair with you. As far as you want."

Lily looked at him.

"Okay," she said.

Devon stepped forward and slapped her in the face, but she didn't move.

Taylor imagined that inside Lily was some kind of glowing core of strength made of a rare outer-space metal that radiated power into all her veins and muscles. She could almost see a halo around Lily's pale face, her dark hair all tangled, her graceful jaw spotted with bruises.

Taylor wished they were alone here so she could just watch Lily.

Lily tried to cross her legs, as if she'd forgotten already

that her ankles were tied, then pulled her cigarettes out of her coat pocket. She lit one and sat at the table making smoke rings, her jaw snapping back each time. Taylor watched Lily's long throat muscles moving where they emerged from her scarf. She wanted to touch that throat, even kiss it. She felt herself blush, and put the thought away.

Taylor had played with girls before, when she was younger. Lots of girls did that. Jennifer Scannell was in her day camp the summer they were eleven, and on an overnight camping trip they pretended to be boyfriend and girlfriend. They smooshed their mouths together, making goofy moaning sounds and calling each other Honey and Darling as all the other girls watched. It was hysterical. The other girls were laughing their heads off and yelling "Ewww."

But she and Jennifer never stopped looking at each other while they were smooshing mouths, and the next morning when they had to get water from the creek, they stopped in a well of shadow under a big tree and gave each other a swift, serious kiss.

Then Jennifer Scannell had a birthday and moved up to Muskrats at the beginning of the next two-week session. The Muskrats had a different swim period and got to take the canoes out. Taylor only ever saw her again in passing.

She'd also seen a film of women kissing and touching. Devon had tried to show her some porn that his older brother had on his computer. The women were naked and glossy, with enormous breasts and huge hair and dangerous-looking fingernails. The whole thing upset Taylor — she wasn't sure why — and Devon turned off the computer. He took her hand and led her out of his brother's room. They went out for fries and she sat sipping her Coke, feeling small and homely with her brown hair and Dollar Store eyeliner.

Then Devon said, "Those women were gross, eh?" and Taylor's mood lifted.

That night she was babysitting Mason while her sister and Bracken were out. Mason was asleep, and Taylor and Devon were making out on her bed. Devon pushed up her shirt and held her small breasts in his hands and kissed them worshipfully, and Taylor wanted to stay with him forever.

Now she thought she could walk away and never miss him again. He was sitting on the counter next to the grotty little sink and swinging his feet, casually kicking Lily each time. Lily didn't try to move her chair away, and Devon's kicks were getting harder.

Taylor willed Lily to react before he really started to hurt her. Taylor had seen with her sister how misplaced courage could end badly.

She stood up and walked over to Devon, sliding next to him and putting her arms around his neck.

"Come sit down with me," she said.

"I have a better idea." He took Taylor's hand and led her to the bedroom, closing the door behind them. He pulled her down on the bed and started to kiss her. She remembered the blunt toe of his boot hitting Lily over and over on the side of her thigh, imagined the dull-blue bruise that must be forming there under Lily's pale, thin skin. But she forced herself to kiss him back, and he was so sweet with her that gradually it became real. They kissed slowly and gently. She touched his face and felt the shape of his jaw, which she had always loved. He stroked her arms and her waist, and eventually slid his hand inside her open coat and up inside her shirt to touch her breasts.

At first his hands were painfully cold, but as they warmed up against her skin, she loved the way he touched her, his finger pads silky and smooth.

Why was it so hard to remember how brutal he was when he was being nice to her? And why was it so hard to remember how it felt when he was nice when he was being mean?

Taylor felt stupid, like a little puppet getting jerked by one string and then the other.

Until Lily started helping her get her biology grade up, she'd never done well at anything in school, and she'd just accepted that she wasn't very smart. Not everyone could be smart. Then, when she began to improve her grades, she let her hopes rise that maybe she wasn't really stupid after all. Maybe she could do something with her life. Maybe she could even give Mason a good life.

She'd let herself imagine Mason growing up into a boy who could do algebra and had friends and played baseball and would get a job after school. A boy who would become a normal man with a regular house and a regular job. Maybe he could even go to university. Her mother had done a year at college before she left to make some money. Then she got pregnant with Tannis and never went back.

Lots of people went to college and university. Maybe she could get her grades up high enough to go to college herself. What did you do with a biology degree? Maybe Mr. Assouad would help her. He thought she was smart, didn't he?

But now she was stupid again. It was too hard to remember things just at the moments when she needed them. Her mind was thick and slow.

This, on the other hand, she could do. She knew how to kiss Devon, knew how he liked to be sucked, knew how to move her hips when he was inside her.

Taylor kept kissing Devon. One part of her mind was paying attention to the pleasure of her lips on his soft warm mouth, the electric feeling of his fingers on her nipple. But another part of her brain was shocked to realize that her life had actually gotten better — at least in some ways — since her sister was murdered.

She had to detach her mouth from Devon's and gasp for breath. She tried to swallow back the tears, but couldn't.

"Dev," she cried, "I miss my sister."

He drew back, surprised, then folded her in his arms and hugged her close, patting her back.

"Whoa, whoa, where did that come from?" he said, stroking her hair.

Taylor couldn't talk. Now that she had a reason, all the sorrow and tension charged through her, pounding her chest from the inside. She saw her sister's corpse again, with the gross stitches being pulled through her gray skin. She thought of Mason alone at home, having nightmares in his dark bedroom. She pictured the big blue ribbon that Mr. Assouad had given her for her Most Dramatic Improvement in biology. She was sure she'd never have another chance for a dramatic improvement.

Devon touched her face, then began to kiss her again. He was like an octopus. She couldn't get away from all his arms, his tentacles, his suckers. She didn't want to touch him, but he was the only thing she knew how to do, and he had her here now.

With an effort, she turned her mind to him. It was like

changing the direction of a big heavy boat, pushing against water. She let herself think about his soft mouth, his cold fingers against her cold skin. Gradually she relaxed and gave herself back to what she now thought of as her job.

Devon stroked Taylor's nipples until they were hard. Then, inside her clothes, her stomach, her hips, her thighs. He nudged her legs apart and ran his fingers over her. She could feel herself damp, her skin electric. He sat up and pulled off her boots and jeans. The cold air against her skin made Taylor shudder. She wriggled under the covers.

As long as she could keep Devon in here with her, he wouldn't be outside kicking Lily.

His boots dropped off his feet and hit the floor. She held the covers up so he could come under. He rolled on top of her and she held him close, kissing him, until she felt him pushing her legs apart with his knees.

"No," she whispered. "We can't do it again without protection."

Devon kept pushing with his knee. He nuzzled her neck.

"Sure we can," he said into the skin of her neck.

"But, Dev, what if I get pregnant? Gram would be so mad. Your father would be so mad!" She could feel him poking at her inner thighs, and she tried to wriggle out of the way.

"It doesn't matter," he said, pulling her hips closer. "We'd just get married."

Taylor felt her heart collapse. As much as she'd been telling herself Devon was all she could do, the idea of marrying him and having a baby with him and having to stay with him forever was unbearable.

She felt him nudging into her, and she moved her hips sideways.

"No, Dev, please," she said, pushing him away. "Let me suck you off, please. You like that." She struggled to keep the panic out of her voice, trying to sit up so she could reach him with her mouth.

"Nope," he said. He pushed her back down and wedged her legs open with one forceful movement of his knees and, steadying himself with one hand, pushed hard into her.

Taylor clutched his shoulders and gasped. It fucking hurt. He started to push, slowly, smoothly.

"No, Dev, no, please," she whispered, still trying to push him away from her.

She wanted to yell, but she didn't want Lily or Conor to hear them.

"Quiet," he whispered, kissing her face.

The thought of having his baby inside her, of being tied to him by a person in her body, terrified her.

"No!" she cried in a loud whisper, urgent, grabbing his hair and pulling his head up and away from her.

He tore his head from her hands and looked down at her, and she saw at once that she'd made a terrible mistake. His face was like thunder.

He lifted one of his big hands and punched her so hard in the jaw that she actually saw stars. Then he laid one bent arm across her chest and held her two wrists in his other hand and pounded himself endlessly into her until he came, uttering a strangled howl into the cold all around them.

Taylor was too tired to hate him. Instead, she pitied him. He sounded like a dying animal.

Eight

LILY TAPPED HER FEET to keep them from falling asleep, and because she had too much energy to stay still. Also because she could see it was irritating Conor, although he was pretending it wasn't. Or maybe he was irritated because they could hear muffled squeaky-bed sounds from the bedroom. It was embarrassing. Plus it meant that Devon was having a good time while Conor was just bored and frozen. If she were in his boots, she'd leave. Instead, he kept launching himself off the couch and pacing the room, rifling through the cupboards or tossing the couch cushions to find his lighter.

Lily had started rationing her cigarettes, and Conor was getting low, too. No surprise. There was nothing to do here but smoke. She wished there was a board game in this place, or some magazines. Didn't people usually have stupid old books in these cabins, like the Hardy Boys or bird guides or something?

She was also getting hungry again, and Conor must be, too. The breakfast donuts and muffins were long gone.

She pulled some bills and change out of her jeans pocket and slapped them down on the table.

"Hey, Con Man."

"Don't call me that," he said in a low voice.

"Whatever." She knew she had his attention. For a few minutes she just played with the change, lining up the coins, then arranging them in a circle.

"What," Conor barked. Lily kept herself from smiling. She used the side of her hand to sweep all the money over to the edge of the table.

"We're gonna run out of smokes. Here, take my money."

She looked up at him, keeping her face pleasant, as if she weren't tied to a chair in a cabin in the middle of nowhere, and he hadn't rammed her head into a car door while re-kidnapping her.

He sauntered over to the table and made a show of counting the cash. Then he pushed the coins into his hand and poured them into a front pocket, folded the bills and pushed them in, too.

He turned and began to walk away.

"Hey, get some food, too. Something good," she said.

He stopped in his tracks and turned around.

"What am I, your fucking errand boy?"

"I'd be glad to go myself," she said, glancing down at the ropes around her ankles.

"Don't be smart."

What a stupid grownup thing to say, she thought. I wonder how many times some adult has said that to him? What does it even mean? Why wouldn't you want to be smart? Why wouldn't your parent want you to be smart?

Well, they don't want you to be smarter than them. Even her retarded mother said it sometimes.

"There's only, like, fourteen dollars here anyway, ya idiot."

Lily shrugged. "That's all I have." She was saving her last twenty for when she and Taylor actually got out of here. It probably wasn't even enough for one of them to get on a bus home, but it was better than nothing.

"I could come with," she said, smiling, so he could either take it seriously or as a joke. If he let her go with him she wouldn't allow the opportunity to pass by again. She felt ready to kill him if she had to.

"Stupid bitch," he muttered. He sat down on the couch and fingered a joint out of one of his pockets. Lily's heart sank. He lit the joint and inhaled, blowing the smoke straight at her. She rolled her eyes and went back to tapping her feet, drumming her hands against her thighs, too.

"Cut it out," Conor said. "What are you, ADD?"

"No," said Lily. She stopped drumming and tapping. "I'm bored. Cold and bored." She held out a hand. "Hey, give me some of that."

Conor snorted. "No."

"You know you shouldn't smoke up and drive."

"Who said I'm driving anywhere?"

Lily held up her almost-empty cigarette pack and shook it.

"This does," she said. "Plus, soon you're gonna need munchies, and there's nothing here. Nada. Zip. Zilch. Zero."

Conor smoked his joint down to the roach, then pinched it off and tucked it back in his pocket. Lily's heart bobbed up again as he zipped his jacket all the way to his chin and slouched out the door.

The room filled briefly with a rush of colder air.

Lily pulled her cell out of her coat pocket and glanced at the time. She would pay attention now. When Conor returned she'd know how long it took to get somewhere from here. Whatever that was, she could figure out how long it would take to walk. That would be some information, at least.

With Conor gone, the cabin felt too quiet. With a glance at the bedroom door, Lily reached down and tried to untie the rope, but the knots were too tight and too far behind the back legs of the chair. She tried picking at them until she hooked a fingernail and it pulled painfully and tore at the cuticle. She sat up again and sucked the bead of blood off her torn finger. Goddamn it.

How ridiculous was it to be alone here and trapped. Well, not completely alone. Lily could hear occasional sounds from the bedroom. On one level, she didn't know how Taylor could stand to sleep with Devon when he was so mean to her. On another level, she knew quite well how that happened. She'd decided for herself that she would rather be alone than be with someone who treated her like shit. She hoped she could stick to that if someone ever wanted to be with her.

Lily tapped her feet. Her boots were still damp and her feet felt like they were shriveling from the cold. She tipped her chair slightly back, holding onto the edge of the table. Then she tipped it to one side, to the other side. She almost lost her balance and grabbed for the table edge.

God, she was bored. She hoped Conor had lots of cash and would show up with a couple of magazines or something. Wasn't there even an old newspaper in here to light the fireplace with? She saw none.

I'll have another smoke, she thought, then not have another one until something happens. Until Conor comes back, or someone comes out of the bedroom. Or...

What else could happen? Nothing.

She slid a cig out of her pack and stuck it in her mouth, then reached for her lighter, but it slipped away from her and hit the floor.

Her heart froze. If it skidded too far away and she couldn't reach it, she wouldn't even be able to smoke!

She waited until the plastic cylinder came to a stop. There, next to the kickboard below the kitchen counter.

She stopped and thought. She pushed the chair back from the table and lowered herself almost to her knees, the rope at her ankles straining. By leaning, she could now reach the lighter. With a huge effort of her leg muscles and an arm bracing herself against the table edge, Lily was able to push herself back up.

Sitting back in the chair, she lit her cigarette, taking a long grateful drag and blowing the smoke out into the cold air of the cabin. She felt such a big sense of accomplishment that it made her giggle a little.

Boredom made you do all sorts of stupid things.

She thought back to the many dim afternoons she'd spent with Jay in his basement, high or coming off a high, half-empty bags of chips or cookies strewn across the floor. They ended up doing silly things. Holding their palms over candle flames. Taking apart Oreos and building little snowmen out of the filling, then using the chocolate wafers in a mini-Frisbee war.

Once, they completely switched clothes, with Lily inside the basement bathroom and Jay outside the door. When Lily emerged and they saw each other, they laughed so hard they could barely stand. Lily wore Jay's gray sweatshirt, which was tight around her breasts but hung to her knees, and his black jeans that were ridiculously baggy on her. He wore her jean miniskirt and her striped knee socks, and his knobby knees stuck out.

Then there were the stupider things they did, like the time in the middle of winter when they started dragging each other around the basement in Jay's plastic kiddie sled, and somehow ended up lying on the carpet, using Jay's lighter to slowly melt the yellow plastic rope attached to the front. The melting plastic smelled so awful that after a few minutes they threw the sled out the back door into a pile of snow, and then had to leave the basement anyway because of the stink.

Lily wanted another cigarette but made herself wait, playing with her lighter instead, flicking it on and letting it go out over and over. They had often done this, or burned bits of paper. One time Jay tried burning a potato chip.

Lily leaned down and idly began to burn off the single fibers sticking out of the rope around her ankles. It took her a few tries to get the angle right.

She had done every loose sticking-out bit on the rope between her ankles and had started on the loops around the outsides of the chair legs, when she was startled. She whipped her head up and looked toward the door of the bedroom, thinking that Devon would accuse her of trying to escape, although she wasn't.

She sat very still, waiting for him to come out the door,

until she again heard the sound that had startled her — a branch pushed by the wind against the window. She exhaled and sank down into her chair, and then, in the next instant, sat up again. She barked out a laugh.

"Fuck a duck," she said under her breath. "What a girl's gotta do."

And she leaned over again to apply her lighter to the rope.

Nine

A GREAT WEIGHT PRESSED Taylor into the ground. She was lying on her back beside a highway, and there was a big rock on top of her. Her chest was being flattened. She wondered if her ribs would break. She struggled to breathe. She didn't know why the rock was pressing down on her. It was hot, maybe from the sun, and surprisingly soft.

Then she began to surface from sleep. She remembered that she was in bed with Devon. She opened her eyes and saw his face flushed pink, a thread of drool at the corner of his mouth.

Taylor tried to wiggle herself around, at least relieve some of the pressure of Devon's weight on her, but he stirred a little and she stopped. Him asleep was the best-case scenario. She could live with the weight for a while.

She breathed shallowly, pushed the muscles of her chest out to the sides to let more air slip into her lungs.

The room was cold and dim. The faded curtains didn't

cover the single window, the glass itself lightly frosted with blown snow crystals — or maybe it was just dust. There was a crack in the ceiling that looked like a man in a square cap with a long pipe sticking out of his mouth.

Why did she think it looked like a man's head? There was no nose or eyes.

Taylor gently opened and closed her jaw, testing. It hurt where Devon had punched her, but it didn't seem to be broken or anything. She used her tongue to feel her teeth and the inside of her cheek. Teeth seemed all intact, cheek was definitely sore. Maybe the inside of it had mashed against her molars when Devon's fist drove the two body parts together.

Flesh healed. It was bones and cartilage you had to worry about. Tannis had accumulated enough permanent injuries that she had started to look kind of battered all the time, even though she was still only in her twenties. Taylor had seen women on the street, in the hospital, with faces and bodies made crooked by years of abuse. Thirty-year-olds who looked fifty, worn and ground down, limping or with one shoulder higher than the other, crooked facial features as if someone had simply remolded them carelessly.

Devon had never hurt Taylor like that. Yet.

Devon's breath was hot and smelled of cigarettes with a milky undernote. His skin had that faint warm, gamey odor. Taylor sniffed it in now. Sometimes she felt she could taste it. It was lovely.

Tears started in her eyes and she felt all mixed up. She looked away and paid attention to the room again. A big wardrobe stood against the wall opposite the window.

For some reason the sight of it suddenly made Taylor

wonder why, if this was Devon's father's cabin, she'd never heard of it before, had never been here.

It was a lie. That's why he had to break in.

On the other hand, she could totally see Devon's father wanting to come to the woods to kill things. It could totally be his dad's gun. She briefly felt guilty for suspecting Devon of lying, then told herself she should suspect him. After all, he'd tricked her into coming here. Just a ride. Isn't that what he said?

She felt his penis in a soft sticky lump against her thigh. Chances were she wasn't pregnant, but she had to get the fuck out of here before he forced her to take more chances. She suddenly wondered whether he was actually trying to get her pregnant, to trap her into marrying him. She closed her eyes again and swallowed.

That, she would not let happen.

Tannis had considered getting an abortion when she found out she was pregnant with Mason. She had already broken up with Mason's father. He was nice enough, didn't hit her, kept a job the whole time they were together. Taylor remembered that he played checkers and cards with her once in a while, although she was still really a kid. He was good at Concentration. But he went off somewhere to find better work — Alberta, maybe — and they let that be the end of the relationship. Tannis hadn't planned to have a baby at seventeen, but she left it too late. Gram was furious. Even Taylor, at ten years old, could see that not choosing was a choice. She vowed then that she would not do the same thing.

When Mason was born, she cuddled him and smelled his sweet baldy head, held the little bottle for him and watched his tiny mouth, and she understood why someone might choose this. It obviously made Tannis feel good for a while. She'd accomplished something, taken on a big project. Made herself truly the center of someone's existence.

After they moved in with Bracken, though, all that seemed beside the point. And then Bracken killed her, and Mason was left with Taylor. That is, they were left with each other.

Taylor carefully lifted an arm and smeared a slow, itching tear out of the corner of each eye. She missed Tannis.

Sometimes at night when Mason was asleep and Bracken was out, Tannis became her old self again, sweet and goofy. They would make popcorn or ice cream sundaes and play cribbage. Tannis would sneak her peg all over the board when Taylor wasn't looking and then laugh her head off when Taylor pretended to be mad. She'd offer to drink the whole bottle of chocolate sauce as a penalty, holding the plastic squeeze bottle over her open mouth and getting chocolate all over her face. One time she squished a maraschino cherry onto the end of her nose, making herself look like a sundae clown.

By the time Taylor started developing, her mom was gone. So Tannis helped her buy her first bra, and showed her what to do when she got her period. She taught her to apply eyeliner and how to use a curling iron. Those were the rare times she wasn't at work, or wasn't too tired, or wasn't with Bracken. When Bracken was there it was as if Taylor barely existed.

Taylor snuffled a little. She couldn't let herself cry if it would wake Devon.

She wondered what Lily was thinking right now. She couldn't hear anything out in the main room of the cabin.

Maybe Lily and Conor had simply gotten disgusted and left. What if she and Devon were trapped here, with no way to get home, nothing to eat? She wouldn't blame Lily for just taking off after Taylor got her into this horrible situation, but...

Devon shifted position, muttered a little, then settled again. Taylor waited, breath held, until she was sure he was still fast asleep, then exhaled.

She was sure Lily wouldn't just abandon her. At least Lily would go back and tell Gram where they were, or something.

Taylor cocked an ear and tried to make out any sounds — the scrape of a chair, the click of a cigarette lighter. Sometimes she thought she heard something, but then it was the wind outside, or a tree branch falling into snow with a dull thud.

Lying here, marooned under Devon's body, with pins and needles starting in her foot, Taylor let herself feel lonely. If she could just shift out from under Devon without waking him, she could go hang out with Lily. Even if Lily was tied up, Taylor could sit there with her and they could talk. They could always find something to talk about. Their families, their ideas for their future lives. Their favorite ice cream flavors, including one Lily made up that would last for days, because it was vanilla crammed with jawbreakers, and you weren't allowed to stop eating it until you had sucked every one of the jawbreakers — no crunching.

That was the greatest thing about Lily. She could talk about anything, she was so smart. Sometimes she could carry a whole conversation on her own, with the two faces on her fingers.

Taylor giggled to herself. She fantasized that she could slip out of bed and go out and find Conor gone. Then she could untie Lily and they could escape. She pictured them stumbling through snowdrifts, clinging to each other, keeping each other's spirits up until they reached a town, or found a gas station, or got a ride from a passing car. Maybe they could just keep running, go somewhere far away and warm, and live together. San Francisco, maybe, where Lily's uncle lived. Or Italy. Why not? They could live in a castle in Italy. Lily could be a world-famous hat designer. Taylor could totally imagine Lily sashaying down some cobbled Italian street wearing an enormous hat made of shiny fabric with huge feathers on it, her white face glowing pale underneath.

And Taylor could run a daycare in their castle where the little Italian kids could learn English. She imagined teaching them the alphabet song. She and Lily would eat pizza every day, except when they had spaghetti. Mason could visit them, and he would love it.

God, she could eat a pizza right now. She wondered if she should try to go out there.

She flexed her right leg and edged it a smidge to the right. She waited a moment, then edged it out a little further.

No reaction from Devon. A little further.

Devon moved again, mumbling. He put his open hand against Taylor's face and then drew it away. Lifting his head, he opened one eye and looked at her. She could see that he was still mostly asleep. She held still. He closed his eye again, one hand in her hair. He began to breathe evenly again.

Anyway, if Lily and Conor were out there, it was still better for Taylor to keep Devon in here. She had a better chance of managing him that way. She had to protect Lily. And in two days it would be Christmas, and someone would try to find them. Or Conor would want to go home. Or Devon would. How would he explain to his parents that he'd missed Christmas? His mother would kill him, and then his father would kill him, too.

This made Taylor feel slightly better. Maybe this was just a two-day trip, like some horrible school outing. She sighed.

She hoped Lily would still want to be friends with her after all this.

Ten

THE SMELL OF POT always made Lily think of hay, though she couldn't actually remember a time when she had smelled hay. Maybe a school trip to a farm, before she was old enough to remember. She had the idea that hay was sort of sweet and grassy, like pot.

The burning rope smelled a tiny bit like hay, or burning leaves in fall. Lily stopped before the rope was burnt through because she worried the smell would bring Devon out. She couldn't decide whether to just finish it and be ready to run, or stop and try to kick the rope apart later.

If only the door to the bedroom would open and Taylor would just step out. Then Lily would quickly burn or break the rope and they'd run out into the snow, or come up with some other plan. Devon had the gun, but maybe Lily could hide behind the door as it opened and whack him with a frying pan.

She hated not knowing what to do. She hated physical

fights and had avoided them since she was a kid. It was humiliating, whether you won or lost.

In grade school she fought some mean kids who figured out that the word "retard" made Lily furious. She never learned how to punch properly, but she was like a crazy windmill with her fists and her feet, pulling hair and biting.

She only stopped when the principal called her mother in. She came into the office where Lily sat, face dirty, wiggling her now much-looser tooth with her tongue. Lily saw the contempt settle on the principal's face as her mother struggled to speak. Her mother turned red and later, at home, smashed the two pretty etched glasses they'd bought that weekend at the Salvation Army store, stomping them and sobbing.

Lily learned to ignore the other kids to save her mother from having to talk to the stupid principal again.

What was she thinking when she got into the car? She should have memorized the license plate number and run into the house to call the police instead.

She chewed a fingernail. Devon scared her. She'd seen enough of her mom's boyfriends to know that Devon was all about being in control.

Lily had really thought that she and Taylor, together, could stand up to Devon. She never expected a gun. One of her mom's boyfriends had a knife, but she'd never even seen a gun before.

She chewed another fingernail. Maybe Taylor was being so passive to keep Devon from hurting Lily. She pulled her finger out of her mouth and laced her two hands together to stop herself from shredding her cuticles.

Were they both giving Devon extra power, trying to protect each other?

What should they do instead?

Lily tried to remember what she'd found in the cupboards when they arrived. There was a tin coffee pot. She couldn't remember a frying pan. There was the poker Devon used to break the lock off the ammo cupboard, but if she didn't knock him out with the first blow, he could easily get it away from her. That would be awful.

Anyway, much as she hated him, she didn't actually want to kill anyone. She didn't want to spend her life in jail, didn't want to murder Taylor's boyfriend. Killing was, as a general rule, bad.

No, the very best thing would be for Taylor to just appear in the doorway, leaving a sleeping Devon behind, and they could make a break for it. This time they'd do a better job of hiding from Conor. Or else they'd work together to overpower him, and drive somewhere where they could get help.

Maybe Devon would freeze or starve while they were gone.

Lily had two cigarettes left. She'd promised herself that she wouldn't smoke another one until something happened, but what if nothing happened for hours? She needed this smoke now, for the sake of having something to do with her hands if nothing else. Otherwise she'd chew her fingernails completely off.

She pulled a cigarette out of the pack and lit it. Maybe she should finish burning through the rope, go over and crack the door of the bedroom and see if she could signal Taylor to come out. Doing something would be better than doing nothing, right? But she didn't want to see them fucking, and she didn't want to embarrass Taylor or make Devon mad.

It would be amazing if Taylor just came out.

Lily drew smoke in, blew it toward the ceiling. She loved the way smoke looked, shaped by her and aimed into the air. Like a temporary sculpture made by her breath.

It was the middle of the afternoon. She had to pee. Conor had stolen a roll of toilet paper from the donut place and it was sitting on the table. Lily had half a mind to burn through the rope just so she could go outside, or use the bucket.

The later it got, the darker and colder it would be. She pictured herself and Taylor lying spooned by the side of the road, frozen, frosted with blown snow, being sniffed by a tracker dog. Or their soggy bodies revealed when the snow melted in the spring. Ugh.

Lily took a drag and blew out smoke rings and watched them waft up to the ceiling, expanding and wobbling until they disintegrated. She sat, head back, looking up at the cobwebs.

Why didn't she have some grownup looking out for her? Why couldn't she count on the basic thing of having someone notice when you're gone?

At one point when her mother was in hospital for some brain-related thing, Lily lived in a foster home. The foster parents were okay, but not very warm. Everything in their house was jumbo-sized. The basement was lined with industrial-style gray metal shelves stocked with huge blocks of toilet paper and paper towels, restaurant-sized cans of beans, corn, tomato sauce. The two chest freezers were filled with plastic bags of Tater Tots, Pogos and blocks of ground meat. The washer and dryer were always running, spewing out piles of identical sheets and towels for the six kids living in the house.

Lily understood why they did everything in bulk, but it made her sad. It was like everyone became the same. Monday night was always chili. Tuesday was mac and cheese made with melted Cheez Whiz and macaroni. (Once it was Cheez Whiz and those corkscrew-shaped pastas, and it was actually exciting.) Wednesday was spaghetti with meat sauce and frozen garlic bread.

It was like living inside a weird factory, everything on a system. Her tenth birthday rolled around while she was there, and she happened to be in the basement before school looking for a new jumbo box of breakfast cereal, and she saw the foster mom pull a frozen cake out of a pile of boxes of frozen cake in the chest freezer.

That afternoon the social worker came and took her to have a birthday dinner with her father. Afterward they went to the hospital and took a piece of cake to her mom from the restaurant. When Lily got back to the foster home, dinner was over, cleaned up and put away, everyone asleep or in their rooms doing homework. When she went to get a glass of water in the kitchen, she found the empty box in the garbage. They ate the cake whether the birthday girl was there or not.

Lily took a last drag and ground out her butt. She remembered sitting in the sunroom at the hospital, her mother slurry from the drugs she was on but smiling woozily at Lily. Her father tired, distant (probably under-lubricated), but smiling briefly whenever he saw her look his way.

Incapable as they were of being good parents, she knew they really wanted her to be happy.

At the foster home she would never go without a meal or clean underwear, was never at risk of being dropped from a height, but no one ever smiled in her direction.

They weren't bad people. They were just busy. They didn't belong to Lily, and Lily never belonged to them. It made her feel so lonely she burst into sobs sitting right there in the molded plastic chair in the hospital sunroom, clutching a pot holder her mother had crocheted for her in occupational therapy. Her favorite color, purple. She remembered looking down at it in her lap. When would she ever need a pot holder? She was in grade five!

Now she looked around the slowly dimming plywood room. Another day was passing and Lily felt sure her mother assumed she was at Jay's or with some other friend. If her mother wasn't just asleep, or sitting in a bar with some man who would overlook her lack of focus for the prospect of a roll in the hay after a few drinks. The foster mother would have noticed that she wasn't home from school four minutes after she was supposed to be there, but Lily cried every day she lived in that house.

There was no winning.

Fuck this. She wasn't going to sit here pretending to be weak and helpless. Besides which, she was dying for a pee. A girl's gotta do what a girl's gotta do, right?

She leaned over and used the lighter to burn through the last strands of the rope, and then worked the knots loose.

Finally she was done. She ought to burn the whole rope. Then Devon couldn't tie her up again. Burn the rope, then pee. Quietly, she carried the rope pieces over to the fireplace.

There was a small pile of wood, plus a couple of log chunks and a few smaller branchy and twiggy pieces.

Lily didn't know much about fires, but it could only make the place warmer. That would be good. And if someone saw the smoke and found them, that would be very good. Devon would be mad anyway when he found out she'd untied herself.

She racked her brain. She'd been a Girl Guide for a couple of months once, just long enough to go on a single camping trip. She arranged the smaller pieces of wood, bigger at the bottom, getting smaller up to the top, then draped the ropes over them. She applied her lighter to the rope and it began to burn through, but it didn't catch fire.

She listened carefully for signs of movement from the bedroom but heard nothing, so she started to walk around the room, looking for any stray piece of paper or other burnable material. She grabbed the toilet roll and slipped into the closet with the bucket, leaving the door slightly ajar for light. The flood that came out of Lily gushed noisily against the metal bottom of the bucket. She hoped Devon wouldn't come out and look for her until she'd pulled her pants back up.

She decided to just leave the bucket in the closet, rather than haul it outside to empty it, in case she made too much noise opening the front door.

She collected the cardboard holder Conor had brought their coffee in, feeling a little triumphant as she pulled it apart. There were still a few little paper bags from the muffins. In a drawer in the kitchen she found the box of wooden matches. How had she forgotten that? And a dirty piece of old newspaper that had been put down to line the floor of the cupboard under the sink. She tiptoed back to the fireplace, careful not to crackle the old newspaper too much, and arranged the cardboard and paper on top of and in between the sticks of wood.

Then, holding her breath, she struck a match.

It took several tries, but finally the match caught, producing a weak yellow flame. She held it to a shred of newspaper and it winked out. She struck another one, with the same result. And a third.

Finally, she made a little stack of six matches on top of the paper pile and lit it with her lighter. These stayed alight long enough to catch the paper.

As she watched, it occurred to her that maybe she should have put the small things underneath and the larger pieces of wood over them. Duh again! An almost invisible blue flame ate a widening hole in a scrap of newspaper, the edges of the hole blackening as they spread outward, tiny flares peppering the flame. Lily crouched, blowing on it ever so gently.

The small flame died, but the fire continued to eat away at the paper. Lily saw the hot spot bypass the cardboard without catching, and she reached in to use her lighter on it. The fire seemed to be finished, and she started again with another match stack.

Bit by bit, with the matches and the lighter, she nursed the fire until it burned on its own, barely. She had the brainstorm of burning her cigarette pack, first removing her last, precious cigarette. The fire was smoky, and still so small she didn't know whether the smoke would be drawn up the chimney, but she didn't care. She sat back on her heels and held her hands out over the tender flame. It was a bit ridiculous — she probably looked like a cowboy on the range or something — but even this little warmth made her realize how cold her hands were.

She looked around. Well, if there was nothing left to burn, she could start feeding the couch cushions or the chair legs into the fire to keep warm.

Thinking this made her feel reckless and strong. Okay, maybe not the couch cushions. That would mean sleeping on the icy floor.

Suddenly she wished she had a pan of Jiffy Pop. Wouldn't Devon be mad if he came out and found her untied and relaxing in front of the fire making popcorn!

She giggled. If they'd come prepared, this could actually have been fun. She wished Jay were here instead of Devon and Conor. She and Taylor and Jay could smoke some dope, make some popcorn. They could have brought marshmallows or something.

Then Lily heard a sound outside and realized that Conor was back. She sneaked a look at her phone. He'd been gone for an hour and ten minutes going somewhere and back again over the snowy road.

She smiled to herself. She and Taylor could manage that, even in the dark and cold.

She remembered learning about China in history class. During the revolution, Mao's soldiers marched some insane distance every day, like fifty miles or something. She and Taylor could get somewhere from here.

She took a deep breath and straightened her back.

Now, something would happen.

Eleven

TAYLOR'S FAVORITE BIRTHDAY present ever was a blonde Barbie that came with a white wedding dress. Her friend Carla in grade one had a grandmother who did alterations at the dry cleaning store, and she made clothes for Carla's Barbies. They were glamorous outfits, cleverly concocted from scraps of satin and lace she saved from work and little bits she crocheted. Among these were three wedding dresses, one for each of Carla's Barbies. An ivory satin gown with bell sleeves and a giant Cinderella skirt, a white silk one with shiny bugle beads sewn around the neck, and a long, narrow, lacy gown with a long train. Irish lace — it was the best kind — off a tablecloth, Carla told her. She knew about these things from her grandmother, who was teaching her to sew. You could see the doll's skin through the holes in the lace.

It didn't matter, of course, as Barbie had no nipples or pubic hair.

Then Taylor's mother and her gram bought Taylor her own Barbie. She thought she might faint from happiness when she unwrapped the present. Her Barbie's dress was more beautiful than any of Carla's, with tiny white sateen roses around the hem and a frothy veil that puffed up out of a silvery tiara. She played Wedding by herself, and with Carla, and with a couple of other girls, until she made a bad swap and lost the wedding gown, ending up with a shapeless mini-dress covered in fat aqua flowers. She imagined that everyone swapped everything back and forth all the time. It never occurred to her that the wedding dress wouldn't come back around to her. But no one would swap her anything good for that stupid flowered dress, and nothing she had was worth the wedding dress that was once hers. She cried over it in her bedroom. At first she was crying over the dress, but what really made her sad was the way she'd let herself be tricked.

Taylor knew two girls who got married right after high school. She remembered the buzzing in the locker room and the cafeteria, the bridal magazines and the cellphone photos of the girls in their dresses and French manicures, their stiff beauty-parlor up-dos. She remembered that as a kid she imagined a wedding for herself, a great big floaty white dress. Everybody fussing over her, a huge sugary cake, bridesmaids in matching outfits.

She couldn't remember wanting a husband. Just a wedding.

Taylor didn't know anyone with a good husband. Gram gave in a lot to keep Douglas satisfied, let him make all the decisions except the ones she could slip by him. Taylor couldn't see how you lived with a man otherwise.

Maybe Mr. Assouad was a nice husband. Taylor imagined him sneaking a handful of red-and-green-wrapped candy kisses into his wife's lunch, hooking a mini candy cane on the strap of her purse while she was in the shower. Giving her a stick-on ribbon for Best Weekday Dinner.

Taylor smiled. She wouldn't mind a husband like that.

Devon stirred on top of her and she tenderly pushed a lock of hair out of his face. He lifted his head up and opened one eye, paused, unstuck the other eyelid and looked down at Taylor. He smiled at her, as if he was surprised to find her there.

"Hi," he said, in a voice still thick with sleep.

Taylor smiled back at him. There was something beautiful, a look of little-boy happiness in his expression.

"Hi, baby," she said, and lifted her mouth a little for a kiss. He wiped the back of his hand across his mouth and kissed her. They stayed like that for a moment, just looking at each other.

At first Taylor thought he was just enjoying looking at her, and it made her feel lovely. Then she started to feel measured. What was he calculating? If she looked good enough? Whether he wanted to fuck her again right now? Her left foot was partly numb with pins and needles.

She shifted her weight a little. He didn't move.

"My foot's asleep. Can I just move it?" she said.

Before he could answer, they heard the sound of the car. Devon's head lifted. He held it rigid, listening. Taylor could see the long tendons of his neck stretched tight inside his skin.

The engine was turned off. There was the sound of the cabin door.

"What the fuck is happening now," Devon muttered. He levered himself off Taylor and out of bed in one athletic movement. He pulled on his jeans and headed for the door. Taylor tried to hurry after him, leaning on the side of the bed as she pulled her jeans on, but she stumbled on her numb foot and split her lip on the bedpost. It jarred her bruised jaw and she couldn't help crying out.

She breathed deep for a minute. Then when the wave of pain passed, she rolled her eyes. What a spaz. It wasn't enough for Devon to smack her face. She had to open her own lip.

Twelve

EVERYTHING SEEMED to be frozen for a moment. Conor
stood inside the door holding a white plastic grocery bag.
He was staring at Lily. At the sound of the car, she'd stood
up and leaned casually to one side of the fireplace. Thin
smoke sifted into the room from the fire.

The poker leaned against the rough stone, an inch from
her hand.

They heard the bedroom door click and it swung open.
Devon was pulling on his jacket. Lily could see him regis-
tering the fire, her standing there. Conor in his jacket and
the bag in his hand.

"What's this?" he asked, striding over and grabbing the
bag from Conor.

"Food. Smokes."

"Who told you to go buy stuff?" Devon demanded. He
spilled the contents of the bag out on the table and began
to sort through it.

"My fuckin' stomach told me," Conor said. He started to open the drawers under the kitchen counter. He drew out a knife and opened a jar of peanut butter and began to untwist the tie on a loaf of bread. Devon watched him.

Conor made himself a sandwich and began to eat it right there where he was standing, great bites of food rolling in his big jaws. Devon made himself a sandwich, too, smearing a wide shiny slick of peanut butter on a single slice of bread and folding it over like a futon.

Lily turned. Taylor was standing in the bedroom doorway. Her lower lip was a bloody, brilliant red blob.

Lily's eyes widened.

"What the fuck!" she blurted.

Taylor looked embarrassed as they all turned toward her. The thick clot of blood was glossy as her lip started to swell.

Devon was standing next to the table, his mouth full, the smell of peanut butter strong in the room.

Lily took a step toward him. Hysteria rose in her chest.

"What did you do to her?" she yelled. She heard the shrieky edge to her voice but didn't care.

Devon stopped chewing for a moment, his jaw hanging open, mashed food on his tongue. He closed his mouth and swallowed with a little difficulty.

"Did I do that, Tay?" he asked. There was something so weird in his tone of voice. Taylor shook her head.

"What the fuck!" barked Lily again. How could she protect Taylor if Taylor was constantly protecting Devon?

"No, Lily," Taylor said, sounding retarded from not moving her lower lip. "I did it. I fell." She could hardly pronounce the words.

Lily felt lost. She wanted to believe Taylor.

Devon seemed to feel the girls watching him. Conor was studying the burning end of his cigarette, but Lily could see the tendons of his throat standing out, outlined under his pale skin.

Where was the gun? She reached back until her fingers touched the poker. It must still be in the bedroom.

"You heard her, I didn't do that to her."

Taylor nodded. "Bedpost," she said, mumbling through her fat lip. There was silence.

"She's fuckin' clumsy," Devon added.

Conor gave a single terse shake of the head, a minuscule movement that echoed in the still room.

Slowly, Devon drew another piece of bread from the bag, then threw the slice on the table and turned to Conor.

"Did I ask for commentary?" he said tightly. Conor slowly raised his eyes and looked at Devon, then returned his gaze to his cigarette, taking a drag, blowing the smoke out directly in front of him.

Behind her back, Lily gripped the poker.

Conor reached over to tap his cigarette on the ashtray on the table, and Devon's hand shot out. He smacked the cigarette out of Conor's hand and took a step forward so his face was right in Conor's.

Lily heard Taylor gasp. She looked over and saw the cigarette butt lying on the wooden floor, burning orange.

Conor's expression didn't change. Lily could hear Devon breathing like a bull. His neck was turning red. Then Conor looked up at Devon and took one long step backwards. He drew the car keys slowly out of his pocket and raised them until they hung, glinting dully, next to his face.

Waves of heat seemed to radiate off Devon. Suddenly, he turned away from Conor, shaking his head.

"You fuck," he said, laughing. Then he whipped back around and pinned Conor against the counter with his elbow up under Conor's chin. Lily could feel her pulse ticking in her head as seconds passed.

Finally Devon released him, turning away again, laughing and shaking his head. Without looking up, he retrieved his slice of bread and carefully began to smear it with peanut butter.

The whole room seemed to exhale.

Lily felt her breath seep out of her. Slowly Conor brought his hand down and pushed the keys into his front pocket.

"I don't need to be here, man," Conor said carefully. "This is not my trip."

Devon swallowed a bite of food and reached over to punch Conor lightly on the arm.

"Don't be a pussy," he said. "Anyway, you do need to be here."

Lily watched them, fascinated. She couldn't figure out what exactly was going on, but she could see that they were jostling for power.

"We only agreed drive up and back. I never said I would go — " he gestured bitterly toward the tiny fire still sending its thin gray smoke into the air, " — fucking camping in the middle of winter."

Devon didn't reply, although Lily saw his gaze flick in Conor's direction for just a second. Instead, he picked up a jar of instant coffee and tossed it toward Taylor.

"Think fast!" he yelled. Taylor's arms jerked up to protect

her mangled mouth. The jar fell short and clunked to the floor at her feet. "See?" he said. "I told you she was fucking clumsy." He drew a cigarette out of the pack on the table and lit it, then sauntered toward the couch.

Lily felt the painful release as her shoulders dropped. She watched as all the pieces shifted. Taylor walked toward the sink, crossing paths with Devon as he approached the couch. She rummaged in the cupboards for something to heat water in, then turned the tap and stood waiting, but nothing came out. Lily loosened her grip on the poker and felt the ache in her hand as blood flowed back into it.

Conor walked over and picked his still-glowing cigarette off the floor, examined it, then drew on it as he returned to his post at the counter. Lily saw the small char mark on the wood.

Conor turned to Taylor. "There's no water, moron. Get some snow from outside."

Taylor pulled her sleeves down so they covered her hands and stood, silent.

"Make us some coffee, Taylor," Devon said. Lily could see the back of Taylor's neck rigid with tension.

"Get some snow from outside," Conor repeated.

"Make us some coffee, Tay," Devon said again. The air in the room was thick and hard.

Lily remembered, when she was about nine, waking up and coming into the living room to find her mother holding a paring knife in front of her, her nightgown torn down the middle, her boyfriend towering over her with his fists clenched. Lily walked into the room, took the knife from her mother, then walked over and opened the front door, motioning with the knife for the boyfriend to leave. Then she ordered her mother to change her nightie and go to sleep, which her mother meekly did. Left alone in the empty living room with the knife, Lily jammed it into the wall behind the couch. It stayed sticking out above her head as she snuggled down into the couch cushions.

She lay there for hours in the dark, watching the dimness of the room washed by shifting patches of light from car headlights moving past the window. She felt calm and empty, the knife handle hanging there in mid-air as if intruding from some other room.

Now she threw the poker to one side, hearing it ring against the stone of the fireplace.

"For fuck's sake," she spat. She brushed roughly past Conor and pulled the pot from the sink. She could see the blank expression on Taylor's face, and she was angry.

Taylor was so fucking passive. How did she get herself into a relationship with Devon in the first place? Lily marched to the door and flung it open, leaving it wide as she scraped a potful of snow from the high carved bank next to the door, packing it in with fury.

Jeez, she had to do everything, didn't she?

She swung back into the room, kicking the door closed behind her, and slammed the pot on the counter.

"For fuck's sake," she said again, not quite under her breath. She knew they were all paying attention to her. She went over to the table and briskly made two peanut butter sandwiches. She slapped one down next to where Taylor was standing.

Packed snow took forever to melt. She remembered that much from Girl Guides. They wouldn't drink anything from that stupid coffee pot for hours. She doubted the gas was turned on for the stove, and that was fine with her. Anything that drove them out of this fucking cabin was very fine with her.

She returned to the fireplace and stood with her back to the room, chewing her sandwich and watching her little orange fire.

|||||

The coffee, bitter as it was, made Lily feel much better. She'd given in and propped the pot in the fireplace on a rusty old metal rack she found under the stove. What a homesteader — Little House on the fucking Prairie. But at least it got hot enough to make the crappy instant coffee Conor bought.

She could feel the heat of the liquid sliding down her insides. That always weirded her out, like an X-ray you felt instead of seeing, showing the heat traveling through you.

Taylor had used the hot water to make cups of coffee for everyone, then went out the front door and refilled the pot for the next batch. Lily stood in the doorway, arms folded against her chest, silently watching. When the pot was really full and heavy, Taylor brought it in. Standing at the counter, she scooped a fistful of snow into a plastic bag for her puffed, broken lip.

Lily felt like an asshole for slamming the pot down in front of Taylor. But Taylor made her so impatient. It was like she was willing to totally give up all her strength. And Devon sucked up Taylor's power like she was his battery, and he recharged by draining her away.

Devon was sitting on the back of the couch, his boots on

the seat. That was Lily's sleeping cushion, now made dirty by Devon's cruddy boots. Selfish fucker.

He was idly tossing a couch pillow back and forth with Conor, who was still leaning against the kitchen counter. They were firing it hard at each other's heads, but since it was just a pillow, they could pretend they didn't really want to whack each other. Taylor stood at the stove trying to sip her luke-warm coffee without touching her lower lip. The couple of big chunks of wood in the fireplace had started to burn, and Lily could see that they would need more if they wanted the fire to keep going. The room was barely starting to feel warmer now.

"Is there any other wood anywhere?"

The throw pillow paused in Devon's clutch.

"Why don't you look around, you lazy bitch," he said.

"Last time I noticed, everyone here has done something except you," she retorted.

Devon heaved himself around and fired the pillow hard at Lily, but she stepped calmly aside and it landed right in the fireplace.

She reached in with the poker and pushed the pillow to one side, so it lay partly on top of one of the burning log chunks. It popped into flame, and a sickly gray smoke rose from it, spreading into the room.

"Nice," she said. "But that's not enough."

"Too fuckin' bad," Devon said. "Be cold."

"Not me," Conor said, drawing himself up. "I'm going home." He didn't move.

"You go home when I say you go home," Devon said.

"I did what we agreed. I'm not staying another night in this shithole." Conor looked calm, but his face was pink and his jaw rigid.

"We agreed we would drive here and drive back. I decide when we leave."

"That mediocre shit was not equal to spending two days of my life in a freezer, asshole," Conor said.

"You owe me, and we agreed drive up, drive back. I decide when we leave," Devon repeated. "Next time buy your shit from someone else — or pay your debts. Anyway, you thought it would be fun. Aren't you having fun?"

Conor slammed his boot back against the kitchen cupboards and Lily jumped. She could see the crescent-shaped dent in the cupboard door from Conor's heel.

Lily imagined that she had a pigeon in her chest. She pictured a gentle hand stroking it, smoothing its feathers. She breathed deep.

"Why didn't you just drive yourself, you fuckin' idiot?" Conor's face was hard.

"I didn't have a car, asshole. You know that."

Lily saw Devon look down, his hands slowly clenching and opening at his sides. The big vein in his neck pulsed.

"This is fucked," Conor said.

Finally Devon looked up. "Don't be mad," he said. It sounded like an order. "You didn't have anything else to do."

"I could've been watching TV in my warm house and eating beef stew instead of this crap," Conor said, jarring the table hard with his foot. It teetered at an angle and then returned heavily upright. The bread and peanut butter slid, but stopped short of the edge.

"Come on," Devon said. "Your fuckin' mother doesn't cook."

Lily could see Conor's thoughts running like mice over his face. Suddenly his foot shot out and kicked the table right over. The table slammed to the floor. In the silence the sound echoed.

"I cook," he said, teeth gritted. "And shut the fuck up about my mother."

"You cook?" Devon said softly. There was a thin, tight silence. "You some kind of a faggot?"

Conor launched himself at Devon so hard the couch toppled, leaving Conor straddling Devon against the backrest, Devon's head on the floor.

Conor's punches were wild, glancing off Devon's forehead or tangling in the collar of his jacket. Devon was reaching up, trying to grab Conor's neck between his hands, but Conor's punching arms got in the way.

Taylor was leaning forward. Her face was pale, except for the vivid blotch of her injured lip and a dark smudge on her jaw.

Lily stepped quickly to Taylor's side and grabbed her arm.

"Come on! This is our chance!" Lily hissed into Taylor's ear.

"No," Taylor cried. She tore her gaze from the boys and looked up at Lily. "I can't."

"Come on!" Lily said, yanking Taylor. She dragged Taylor across the floor, avoiding the grunting fighters. "Let's just go!" She yanked Taylor again, hauling her almost to the door. Taylor seemed to inflate herself, and jerked her arm away from Lily.

"Leave me alone," she screamed. "I can't!"

Lily couldn't believe it. Fury rose up through her like a boiling geyser.

"You fucking selfish bitch!" she yelled, and watched,

stunned, as her hand shot out and slammed into Taylor's cheek.

Taylor staggered backwards, then leaped at Lily, slapping her face with a wide-open hand so hard that Lily's head whacked to one side, the skin of her face burning.

They stood and stared at each other forever. Lily had a crazy urge to laugh with joy at Taylor's strength, but she knew she had to move, now. She spun around and headed for the door.

She had just flung it open when she felt herself pulled back by her Most Impressive Scarf. Devon rammed his fist into her stomach and she doubled over, a ragged cry forced up from her lungs. He kicked her and she fell and he slammed his booted foot into her side, over and over, slamming it, swinging back, slamming it. She wanted to slide away from him but her back was already up against the door. She lay curled, eyes shut. All she knew was the force of his boot into her body, over and over. Part of her mind wandered, detached, curiously considering what she could do to make it stop, but it couldn't think of anything.

She knew a kick could rupture something. A kick could injure your brain and make you try to pull your raincoat on over your leg for the rest of your life.

You could be kicked to death.

Suddenly, she refused to let Devon kill her. She summoned all her power and heaved herself out of the way of his next kick, and then felt her eyes pop open wide as there was a flash of silver and Devon swayed, then collapsed to his knees. His face was strangely blank.

There was a great vacuum of silence in the room as Devon fell, in slow motion, like a giant tree. His face hit the floor with a muffled thump.

It was like the world had stopped in its spin, and everything was suspended.

Thirteen

TAYLOR HEARD A ROARING. It was like standing inside all the wind in the world. It filled her head to bursting and she was scared, because anything could be happening around her and she wouldn't know it. She couldn't hear anything but this massive white noise. It was pressing in on her skull from all directions.

Her eyes were stuck, too. She couldn't think of a way to move them from the heap of clothes on the floor. She just couldn't puzzle out where she was and what she was looking at.

And then she understood that the heap of clothes was Devon, lying there face down, and Taylor thought he must have grown, because she could see a white sliver of skin above his sleeve, with the bump on the side of his wrist sticking out like there was a marble under there.

Then the roar in her head began to fade and a thumping replaced it, her own blood thudding through her temples like a series of bowling balls.

Why was Devon just lying there? He looked like a dork. Why couldn't she remember how he got there? And then she realized her hand was killing her, and she knew that she had whammed Devon on the side of the head with the snow-heavy coffee pot, and her fingers had been jammed inside the handle, and suddenly she thought that she had probably broken a couple of them.

Now she remembered thinking, He's going to kill her, I can't let him kill her — and grabbing the first thing she saw, and then swinging as hard as she could.

Her fingers fucking hurt. She thought, I'm going to have to learn to hold a cigarette in my left hand.

Then the room expanded and she saw Lily staring at her from the floor where she was on her knees, hunched over and holding herself, her face whiter than Taylor had ever seen it. And Taylor knew that Conor was somewhere behind her and she could smell his rank sweat and hear his breath coming in and out of him as if his lungs were bellows.

Her whole body turned cold and her muscles turned to water. She dropped to her hands and knees. With a great effort she stayed up on her knees, unsteady, and one side of her mind thought, Maybe this is what happened to Devon. He just can't get up.

The other side of her mind said, Devon's dead. You killed him.

Fourteen

AFTER LILY'S MOTHER came out of rehab, she spent a lot of time with a boyfriend she met there. Neil must have been muscular once, but now looked like a chicken leg left in the oven too long, the meat dry and clinging to the bone. He was a little off — moody and unpredictable, like Lily's mom. But Lily figured that was what her mother liked about him. She didn't need to feel self-conscious about her weird behavior when she was with him.

Lily's mom's speech was slow and difficult, but she would eventually say what she was trying to say. She sometimes said the wrong word, but Lily usually knew what she really meant. Neil always said totally the wrong thing — "teacup" for "newspaper," or "bacon" for "bathtub." He also had trouble remembering words, and would get stuck, his face getting redder and redder.

Lily's mom would go out on the town with Neil, tiptoeing out the door with a finger held up to her mouth, lipstick running over the edges of her lips, to signal Lily not to tell anyone.

Lily knew her mother wasn't supposed to leave her alone, but she loved it. She would wait until she heard the sound of the cab pulling away, and then she would twirl around in the middle of the living room, her bare feet on the matted carpet, the hem of her nightgown belling out. This was her ritual, the sign that she now owned the space. Then she would do any ordinary thing, but it always felt wonderful. She would do her homework at the kitchen table, carefully sweeping up the little eraser turds in her hand and brushing them into the flip-top garbage can. Or if there was no homework she would watch TV and eat saltines with peanut butter, or read Nancy Drews she got for fifty cents each at the second-hand store and resold for a dime. When it was time for bed she would go into her room and sit cross-legged with the covers pulled up over her knees and continue to read. But she never went to sleep until her mother and Neil got home and Lily could see what mood they were in.

Sooner or later they would come crashing through the front door, laughing and shushing each other, or arguing. Sometimes they would unfold the pull-out couch right away and then Lily would roll over, draw the pillow over her head and drop off to sleep to the rhythm of the springs. Other nights they would sit in the living room drinking cans of beer, Neil talking and getting more and more frustrated with his words, or, worse, not speaking.

On those nights Lily lay clutching the sheet until she heard the voices rising or the sound of empty beer cans hitting the wall, or a lamp being knocked over. She strained to hear, from moment to moment, when she might need to run in and get between them so Neil stopped hitting her mother — or, at worst, call 911. She only had to do that once, and it gave her no joy to see the cops hauling Neil away.

After the door closed behind them, Lily's mother sat crumpled in the middle of the living-room floor, holding one of Neil's socks against her bleeding nose. Lily went to her bedroom and locked the door behind her. Before that she would have run around finding her mother ice packs and Aspirins and making her a gin and tonic. This time she climbed into bed with *Password to Larkspur Lane*. She read it with a flashlight under the covers, so her mother wouldn't see the light under the door and try to talk to her.

Now Lily said, "He's still breathing, but it's weak." Taylor looked stunned. Lily sat back on her heels and wiped a hand across her face. She gave Taylor a small grin. "You sure gave it to him, Supergirl."

Taylor and Conor, who stood behind her, still breathing too hard, just stared.

Lily wanted them to get it together. She knew she could be calm and figure out what to do, but every movement was painful. She wasn't carrying that asshole. She couldn't. Every breath sent a knife into her side.

"You. And you. Breathe." She closed her eyes and felt all her aches and pains with her mind, gingerly.

Conor's face was slowly getting paler. It was almost as white as ice. Lily willed him to stay with it. She couldn't take care of anyone else right now.

She focused on holding her insides together while she tried to get to her feet. Every tiny movement revealed new pains. She stopped and breathed — not too deeply because that hurt, too.

"Get the blankets," she said. Taylor glided away, reappearing with a bundle of bedding in her arms.

"Lay those out on the floor and the two of you shift him over onto the blankets and wrap them around him. We have to keep him warm and we have to avoid moving him too much." Vague notions from middle-school first aid came crowding into her mind. "He's probably in shock." She couldn't remember whether you were supposed to elevate the feet or the head in cases of shock, but it was the opposite if there was a head injury.

She supposed, now that she thought about it, that Devon had a head injury.

She almost laughed. A head injury.

Taylor was heaving Devon over onto the blankets bit by bit. Lily watched her holding Devon's huge boots in her hands.

Conor still hadn't moved. Lily summoned her strength to speak firmly to him.

"Help her, Conor. We have to get him to a hospital."

She watched Conor's lips moving slowly.

"He's alive?" Conor said.

"So far," Lily said, "but we have to go. Now." Putting urgency into the "now" sent a stab of pain through her side. Conor moved slowly over to the blankets and began to tug the edge under Devon's shoulder.

Lily scanned the room. They should put out that fire before they left.

Then she set her mouth in a grim smile.

Nah. Let this fucking hole burn to the ground.

Fifteen

As the car pulled away from the cabin, Taylor turned her head and saw light spilling out of the open door onto the trampled snow outside. It looked almost cheerful inside, even though she could see overturned furniture, food wrappers and dirty paper coffee cups through the slot of the doorway.

In the car, she leaned over Devon. The three of them hadn't spoken, carrying him out in his roll of blankets, a pillow from the bed stuffed under his head, all of them holding their arms out under him like zombie medics. Taylor, holding Devon's head, automatically slid into the back seat, scootching across as Lily and Conor fed the length of his body in after. She adjusted his head tenderly across her lap. She saw Lily slide carefully into the front, wincing.

Just before the cabin disappeared behind them, Taylor saw a plume of sparkling snow rise on the wind and scatter across the doorway like a handful of tiny sequins. The door swung on its hinges, back and slowly forth.

She was seized by a fierce hope that the whole place would fill up with ice and snow. In ten thousand years no one would know it had been there, or that anything had ever happened there. In ten thousand years no one would know she, Taylor, had ever existed.

It was a comforting thought. Whatever she had lived through — whatever was to come — it would all be long, long over, thoroughly erased, in ten thousand years. Even sooner.

She held her open palm over Devon's mouth. There was a faint hush of breath against her skin. He was cold and very heavy across her legs. His body twitched restlessly. She could see the shapes of his arms pushing against the blankets. The pillow was squished up against the side of the door, and Taylor leaned her cheek against the top of it, her chin grazing Devon's hair. Very gently she touched her broken lip with the tip of her tongue and felt the seam beginning to form there.

Sometimes when he insisted on pushing into her before she was ready and it hurt, she would tell herself that her pain didn't matter. There was a whole world busy existing all around her — someone walking down the sidewalk outside the window, thinking about what to make for dinner, or what to wear to the club tonight. They didn't know Taylor existed. For them, her pain didn't exist, so they didn't care about it.

If they didn't care, why should she?

She blinked and lifted her head off the pillow. Her cheeks were wet and it was making her face cold. Devon's face was pale and still. His eyebrows were dark brown and feathered across the ridges over his eyes. She had loved lying in bed and barely touching those eyebrows with her fingertips. A wash of moonlight passed through the car and she marveled at how small the hairs were, how they lay in fine and perfect rows, each hair arching over his skin, tracing out the bony ridges underneath.

They had learned in school about how the eyes of many creatures were sunken to protect them, and Taylor would lie with Devon after making love and imagine his eyes were looking out from inside these caves, from under bony overhangs that would deflect flying baseballs, or his father's big grease-stained fists.

It was part of loving Devon, taking this minute inventory of his parts, imagining the life of them. She'd done the same with his nose, a single pale brown freckle on its side in the little fold behind the curve of his nostril. She'd done it with the fine hairs at the back of his neck, the crumpled little white scar shaped like a jammed staple underneath his chin from when he fell out of his highchair as a baby. She ran a fingertip lightly down the side of his cheek, over the very fine down on his upper lip.

She was getting ready to give this up. She didn't know how it would happen, whether he would die or whether she would be sent to some juvenile institution for cracking him with the coffee pot, or something else, but she knew it would happen somehow.

She saw in her mind's eye the old tin coffee pot swinging through the air. Her arm muscles remembered lifting the thing high enough to slam it against Devon's head. She saw her eyes and her brain calculating the arc of the blow, remembered telling herself she had to make this one work or Devon would leave off kicking Lily and turn on Taylor and kill her. She had an image in her mind of Tannis waking up the morning after a bad beating, her eyes almost swollen closed, discovering new damage with each movement of her fingers, arms, trying to lift herself out of bed. Taylor standing beside the bed, dressed for school, holding a cup of coffee under Tannis's chin so she could sip it, and Tannis trying to get up, testing to see if she could stand, what was broken where.

Tannis lived with so much pain and fear, but she never seemed to want to give up. She clung to what was good in her life — to Mason, to Bracken's good days, to winning $500 in the lottery pool at work — to the idea that it wouldn't always be like this.

Well, she got that right.

Taylor thought if it was her she would want to just stop hurting. She wondered sometimes if things would eventually come to that with her and Devon. But then again, Tannis had Mason to think about. Well, now she had Mason, too.

That made her remember that maybe Devon had already made her pregnant, and her stomach heaved a little as if she could throw the little seed up, and she hated him. Then she saw the coffee pot flying through the air again, saw it smash into his head, imagined the wide look of surprise on his face for a second before he collapsed, and then she saw Bracken's beefy arm smashing the portable phone into Tannis's face, and Taylor felt a terrible sick heaviness fill her whole insides.

This is what she had become.

She heard the click of a lighter and the sound of an intake of breath, and Lily handed a cigarette back to her. Taylor felt it had been a year since she'd had a smoke, and she was crazily grateful to Lily. She took the cigarette, her fingers still stiff and hurting but definitely not broken. She inhaled and the smell comforted her and she inhaled again, feeling she might never get enough smoke inside herself. It helped push away that sick feeling.

She saw Lily hand a lit cigarette over to Conor. He took it, and Taylor saw his hand tremble. Then he, too, sucked deeply, never moving his eyes from the road.

Taylor was surprised. She'd been thinking of all this as something Devon had created and was doing to her, and she'd been thinking of Conor and Lily being outside it somehow.

But Conor and Lily were in this, too. Maybe Conor would get the shit beat out of him at home for disappearing overnight, or for getting in trouble. Devon's dad broke Devon's arm once for scraping the side of a customer's Porsche against the wall of the garage while he was moving it into one of the bays.

Now that there was a rush of nicotine in her bloodstream, Taylor suddenly felt hungry. She thought about the pizza kit. It was like thinking of something that had happened in Ancient Egypt — forever ago, on another continent. She imagined Mason sitting at the kitchen table with Gram, Mason painting sauce onto the elastic dough. Gram supervising from the stove, a cigarette in her mouth, while she fried something for Douglas.

Was Mason fidgety when Taylor and Lily didn't come in for dinner? Did he scream when he was put to bed, or did he fall asleep, his little stomach full of pizza dough and cheese? Maybe Gram sat on the bed with him. She hated doing that. It felt like a waste of time to her, but Douglas wouldn't have put up with Mason crying.

It was all about taking care of the person above you in the chain of command. The thought made Taylor's shoulders slump.

She cranked down the window and a wall of cold hit her in the face. She pitched her butt out and sparks flew back into the night. She cranked the window closed as fast as she could. She put her hand near Devon's mouth to make sure he was still breathing, but his lips were almost closed, so she licked her finger and held it under his nose. A faint brush of air came out lukewarm.

Devon seemed to be conscious now, but his eyes were heavy. He looked dozy.

"Dev?" she whispered, but he didn't respond. Taylor wondered if she should be trying to keep him awake. She had to do that for Tannis a few times when Bracken gave her concussions.

She nudged Devon's cheek gently. He unstuck his eyes and turned his head a little to glare at her. She couldn't risk getting him riled up. She imagined him rising up and grabbing her head and smashing it against the car window. She imagined her head split like a pumpkin on the sidewalk the day after Halloween.

She let him roll his face away, and his eyelids slipped down until only a pale line remained visible.

If he died in her lap, she wouldn't have to worry about him anymore.

Suddenly she remembered that tomorrow was Christmas. Would she spend the day in jail, alone?

She'd planned to do her Christmas shopping today, and now she would have nothing to give anyone. She was going to get Mason one of those round plastic sleds like a giant contact lens that you could use to go down the side of a hill or to pull a small kid along an uncleared sidewalk. She imagined Mason sitting between her legs, his cheeks red with cold, sliding down the snow like happy people. And she was going to get Gram some nice soap — something that would smell good, something she'd never get for herself. And there were those earrings for Lily.

It made Taylor's heart ache to think of how she'd planned to buy those earrings for Lily, and how much everything had changed since then.

Sixteen

LILY GAZED OUT AT the black forms of bare tree branches like a tangled shadow stencil. The snow on the edges of her Most Impressive Scarf had melted and made the wool damp and scratchy against her neck. Even the touch of her scarf against her skin was almost a kind of pain, and there, there was that stabbing in her side again.

Lily wondered whether her mother tried to escape the pain of her transformed brain by thinking outside herself, too. Maybe her handicap made it harder for her to do that. How awful not even to be in control of your own thoughts.

On the other hand, who was in control of their thoughts, really? Once her mother burst in the front door sobbing with rage, her open coat flapping. She ran straight to the kitchen, grabbed the porridge pot from the back burner of the stove and, with a great cry, slammed it full into her own face. Lily had crept over and held her mother around the shoulders as she lay on the floor, crying with her whole heart. After she emptied herself of tears, Lily's mother accepted a sippy cup of tomato soup, sitting at the kitchen table tipping the cup to her mouth while Lily tenderly held an ice-filled washcloth to her purpling eye. Lily put broken pieces of saltines between her mother's lips, crumbs flecking her chest as if her broken heart had shed bits of itself there.

When the soup was all sucked back, Lily's mother stood and lurched to the cupboard, clumsily twisting the top off the unrinsed sippy cup and pouring a slug of gin straight in.

As she became animated with the warmth of the alcohol, the story came out. Lily's mother, having lost her job mopping the floors of an office building, had tried to fill out a form for welfare, but since her accident her writing had become almost illegible. Her words crawled over the page — letters jumbled, numbers appeared in the margins when they ought to have been on dotted lines. And when the woman in the welfare office asked Lily's mother to sign her name, her mother drew a tangle of circles and crooked lines. The woman asked her to sign again, and then again.

Lily could picture her mother's face knotted with the effort of concentration, the dark look coming into her eyes when effort slipped over into slow-burning fury.

Lily had seen this before, over a load of laundry that ended up in balls instead of folded, over a pan full of chicken that her mother was trying to fit into the cutlery drawer. At the welfare office Lily's mother shouted, pounded her fist on the counter, finally threw a wastebasket. The security officers bundled her out of the building and wouldn't let her come back in. Somewhere along the way she lost a shoe and cut her heel.

Sitting on the floor, cradling her cup of gin against her

chest, she sobbed, her breath a strange cloud of alcohol and half-digested tomato.

The car seemed to be slowing, grinding over the gritty frozen snow furrows on the shoulder. Lily wondered if there were ditches by the side of the road here. Maybe they would roll into one and be stuck. She glanced out the window but couldn't see enough to tell. No distant houses, no signs, no headlights in the distance.

The car came to a stop.

In the darkness there was silence, then sounds emerged. The wind threw itself against the car, tossing silvery veils of snow that sounded like metal filings along the sides of the vehicle.

Someone was tapping something. Conor. His hand was shaking, and the button on his jacket cuff was hitting something metal on the car door.

Lily's whole body sank. She didn't have enough strength left to be in charge of one more thing. She couldn't do it. So she just sat.

She knew they were waiting for her to say something. The fuckers. They would sit here all night and freeze to death if it was up to them.

She hated them. Devon and Conor most of all, but Taylor, too.

She felt like getting out of the car and starting to walk, even if the wind scoured the life out of her and left her a shell on a crusty snowbank somewhere. Just to be alone and not have to worry about anything except how to put one foot in front of the other, over and over, until she got too cold to care.

Lily could hardly feel her fingers. Even in the heated

car her hands just wouldn't get warm. She'd forced her index finger through a loose stitch at the top of her mitten so she could smoke without taking the mitten off, and the wool smelled like burnt tobacco and a trace of wet animal. The smell was half repulsive and half comforting. She kept passing her mittened hand under her nose and sniffing, enjoying it filling her nose but also thinking each time that it was disgusting.

She slid her phone out of her pocket. Even outside a service zone you were supposed to be able to get 911. Maybe they could get an ambulance to meet them on the road. She pressed the On button, but nothing happened. She pressed it again and waited. The phone was a silent little black wafer.

Her charger was on her bedside table. She could picture it. Next to her yellow plastic water glass with Tweety Bird on it and her ashtray and her little reading lamp that always reminded her of a bent-over stork. For a moment she wanted to cry, then was surprised to find that she was almost relieved.

It made things simpler.

It was still dead quiet in the car. These fucking fuckers would really sit here all night. She wanted to smack them.

She took a breath.

"What," she said. Conor moved his arm, and his jacket button stopped tapping the door.

"I don't want you mentioning me," he mumbled. Silence. Lily heard Taylor rustle in the back.

"What?" Lily said tiredly.

"I'll drop you somewhere, then I'm getting out. And don't mention that I was even here," Conor said. "That I was part of this."

"Fine," Lily said. "Now just drive."

"No!" Taylor cried from the back seat. "It's not fair!" There was a high edge to her voice. Lily turned with difficulty, trying to see Taylor's face in the dark.

"It's okay, Taylor," she said. "It doesn't matter."

"Yes, it does!" Taylor yelled. "We didn't want to come here. You made us! Devon made us and you helped him!"

Taylor was leaning forward, her coat front almost covering Devon's face.

"He kicked the shit out of Lily, and you let him! You drove us out to the middle of fucking nowhere! My dead sister's kid's gonna be alone on Christmas because of you!"

Then she burst into tears, reaching across and bringing her fist down hard on Conor's shoulder.

"You asshole!" Taylor cried, her voice hoarse. She sank back into her seat. Conor didn't even turn around.

"Taylor," Lily said. She could hear herself using the voice she used with her mother. Conor had his head bent, and his hands clutched the sides of the steering wheel. Taylor snuffled and then passed the back of her coat sleeve across her nose.

Lily wasn't sure what Taylor was freaking out about exactly, but she didn't want Conor to get so spooked he wouldn't drive.

"It'll be okay, Taylor. I promise."

Lily lit another of Conor's cigarettes and passed it to Taylor, then another one for Conor. He lifted his head to take it.

"Drive," she said, her voice low and calm.

In the quiet inside the car Devon coughed, then gave a low moan. Conor started the car and Lily felt the engine working to haul them forward onto the road. She pulled for it in her mind. When the wheels slid past the icy shoulder and caught on the road surface, a small motor turned over in her chest.

They couldn't be far from somewhere now. Soon they would be on to the next thing, whatever that was. Cops or hospitals or social workers. It wouldn't be fun. But maybe she'd be home with her mother tomorrow for Christmas, and maybe her mother would focus just long enough so they could eat a meal together.

Last weekend Lily had bought the smallest turkey she could find, and potatoes, and gravy mix, and cranberries for homemade cranberry sauce, which her nana used to make for holidays. Lily could still cook everything tomorrow. She planned to eat so much turkey and potatoes tomorrow she'd have to wear her Tweety Bird nightshirt to the table so she could leave her jeans all unzipped.

The car moved along through the night. They followed a curve in the road, and in the distance Lily saw what looked like a star hanging at the horizon, and she wished on it, to get home soon.

A minute later she realized it was lights. She turned slowly in her seat and waited for a moment to catch Taylor's eye. When Taylor looked at her, face puffy in the shadows, Lily smiled at her, and winked.

Seventeen

As the lights of the parking lot washed over them, Devon began to push against the blankets. His voice was low and angry.

"Let me the fuck up, bitch."

"We're almost there, Dev, hold on. Stay in the covers and stay warm. We're here already, baby." She kissed his forehead and he shook his head furiously, as if trying to throw off the imprint of her lips.

"Get off me!" he said. Taylor had the idea that he thought he'd yelled it, but his voice was trapped in his throat and came out froggy.

And now the car was swinging out of the parking lot again, and Lily had grabbed the steering wheel and was yelling at Conor. Lily wrenched the steering wheel to turn the car back, crying out with the effort, and Conor pulled it back, the car switching back and forth like a mad cat's tail. Lily grabbed a handful of Conor's hair and yanked him backwards. Then she reared up in her seat and brought her face very close to Conor's, her other hand pulling down on her side of the steering wheel.

"Drive. Back. In," she growled.

Conor strained forward against Lily's grip. Lily was making weird whimpering sounds, but her face stayed fierce.

Finally Conor pulled the car into a far corner of the parking lot. Lily pulled his head toward her by the hair and, through gritted teeth, said, "Now. Get out." Conor slowly opened the door and started to slide out of his seat, then stopped and turned.

He looked Lily full in the face, his expression hard as rock, then horked and spat right between her eyes. Then he was gone.

The last Taylor saw of Conor was him hiking fast across empty parking spaces, pulling a cellphone out of his jeans pocket. It glinted dully for a moment in the dim light. Then he disappeared into the darkness at the edge of the parking lot.

She stared at the darkness for a moment, then glanced over at the Tim Hortons coffee shop. It took her a moment to understand that she was looking at a police car, parked right in front.

"Lily," she said. Devon was struggling to sit up. The open car door up front was letting in tons of cold air, and Lily was sitting in the draft, wiping the gob off her face and smearing it on the car seat, her face wrinkled up in a strange crooked way.

"Lily," she said louder. Lily turned and looked at her, wincing. Taylor pointed.

"I know!" Lily yelled angrily. She was rubbing her face with her Most Impressive Scarf.

Taylor thought, everyone here is angry. Then she felt her head bounce backwards.

"Get me out of here, you fucking bitch!" Devon was yelling. His arms were tangled in the blankets but he had freed an arm and, deliberately or not, had driven a fist into the side of Taylor's head. His legs were kicking against the blankets, which were slowly falling away.

"Dev, let me help you," she said, automatically using her soothing voice. "Baby," she said, "I'll do it."

"Where the fuck are we?" Devon was yelling. He turned to Taylor as she peeled the blankets away from him. "You're gonna get it so bad when we get home," he said, holding his white face right up in front of hers.

"Baby," she whispered. He sat up and shifted off her lap so he could reach over and untangle his feet. His movements were slow and heavy. Taylor saw the door handle out of the corner of her eye. She grabbed the handle, feeling the cold metal against her palm as she leaned against the door and slid out. She felt Devon pull on the back of her coat but she kept moving and got free. She took a breath and then ran for it, her eyes on the door of Tim's.

It took her a day, a week, forever to get across the parking lot. She had never done anything so slowly in her life. Her feet slapped against the dirty, gravel-flecked snow as if she was kicking into the outer edges of space, her legs taking an eternity to move forward.

By the time she got to the front door it was as if she had been in another universe for so long that she couldn't make sense of the physical arrangement of atoms on this planet. A wide shining sheet of something hard blocked her way, and yet she could see through it. A flow of weird harsh light came at her. And then she watched as her hands grasped the door and pushed it and pulled it and it moved, and she suddenly remembered how this worked and threw her body into the opening it made. She pushed herself through the inner door and stood in a kind of humming of suspended motion, looking wildly around for a uniform.

There. Taylor ran over and stood before the officers, her chest heaving uncontrollably. Now she realized Devon had been yelling at her the whole time she was running across the parking lot, and she knew he would be here in seconds.

"My boyfriend." She gasped for air as she struggled to remember what to tell them.

"I killed him," she cried.

She turned her head as he crashed through the doors.

Eighteen

LILY WAS SUNK IN her pain. It was as if all the tender places in her body that had begun to knit together were torn open again while she wrestled with Conor. She thought she couldn't stand it. Then she kept standing it even though, each moment, she was stunned by the agony.

Had Devon ever kicked Taylor like he'd kicked her? Or had he just snapped in the cabin?

Lily heard him screaming at Taylor, and the sound of him blundering into the door of the restaurant. But at the time she was sinking onto the frozen slush, and only feeling grateful for the ground. Maybe lying on the snow would be like applying a full-body ice pack. She lay there and thought of her mother, and how she had never understood how much pain her mother probably went through every time she got beat up. Then she thought of how close she was to a hot, sweet coffee.

Lily lay on the ground in the snow, an end of her Most

Impressive Scarf between her cheek and the slush, wetness gradually soaking through. She tried to keep her breaths shallow, because it hurt less. She felt guilty for not going to see whether Taylor was okay, but she was so tired.

Little as she wanted to move, it occurred to Lily that she could die of hypothermia if she lay here all night. She had a vague idea that one of the symptoms of hypothermia was that you stopped caring whether you were cold. Her feet and hands felt so cold now that it hurt, so maybe she didn't have it. Either way, she knew that she ought to get up.

She wondered why you always read stories about people who braved incredible odds, or lived with years of awful suffering, determined to survive. Like Mr. Peterson had made them read that Anne Frank book in World History. And the people in the concentration camps. Why was surviving considered a better idea than letting go of an unbearable existence? What was the point of suffering?

Maybe it was an evolution thing. If every creature who had a hard time gave up, there would be nothing here but bacteria.

She imagined everyone on earth who didn't want to suffer just evaporating. People who had terrible pain from cancer or a car accident. People like her mother who cried every day or lay in bed for hours, weighed down by life.

Lily felt a twinge of guilt, imagining her mother evaporating, imagining she could come home to the apartment and find the bed empty, the sheets still wrinkled around her mother's body shape, and never have to worry about her anymore. Never have to come home and find the shampoo bottle bobbing in the toilet bowl, or the flame of the back burner burning merrily away all by itself.

Lily's face was stiff from the cold, and the socket around the eye that was lying in the slush ached.

She did not want to evaporate. She didn't know why, but she wanted to get up and not die of hypothermia.

Slowly, against the pain in her side, she shifted herself over and was beginning to raise herself from the ground when she saw the ambulance pull in.

It seemed like days later that the officers wrestled Devon to the ground outside the front doors. Lily heaved herself slowly to a sitting position and watched Devon fight back wildly. The two men struggled to subdue him. They finally loaded Devon onto the gurney and strapped him down, Devon still ranting and straining to sit up.

Then Taylor appeared in the doorway of the restaurant and pointed across the parking lot. The cops' heads turned toward Lily. The two figures detached themselves and strode across the parking lot.

In the cop car they made her strap in, which hurt where it cut into her side, but at the same time it made her feel weirdly safe. Taylor strapped herself into the middle seat and cuddled up to Lily, patting her small shoulder to tell Lily to rest her head on it. Lily hesitated — since when was Taylor in charge? — then let herself, shifting gingerly in her seat until she could bend her head to the side.

When the car pulled out, Taylor slipped her cold hand into Lily's, and they held onto each other without moving.

Nineteen

THE LITTLE TREE WAS ALL white, with blue lights and little blue balls hanging from it. Gram and Douglas had put it up in front of the living-room window. It made Taylor think of a figure-skating outfit. There was a crooked hand-made star on top, made by Mason at Trevor's house, shedding red and green glitter onto the branches.

She hadn't got home until six this morning. The police questioned Taylor and Lily separately, and asked Taylor a lot of questions about her relationship with Devon. Then they wanted to send her to the hospital, but she convinced them that her split lip was her own fault.

Gram picked her up at the police station. She gave Taylor a brief hug and then walked her outside without saying anything.

Taylor didn't know if Gram was mad. Maybe she thought Taylor had gone with Devon on purpose, or thought she knew Devon was coming. Or maybe Gram felt guilty for not making Taylor come inside when she saw Devon was out there.

Not that Taylor held it against her.

Gram opened the front door, moving the key slowly in the lock to keep it from echoing in the silent house, turning and putting her finger to her lips, moving her eyebrows in the direction of the stairs.

Inside, she led Taylor to the little white tree. Wrapped gifts were piled underneath. Gram leaned over and pointed at a flat, blue-wrapped box. Taylor looked at the tag. *To: Douglas. From: Taylor.* "Chocolates," Gram mouthed. She pointed to another box. *To: Mason. From: Taylor.*

In the kitchen, Gram handed Taylor a box of pancake mix and started rummaging in the fridge, pulling out eggs and milk and bacon. Taylor got busy mixing batter while Gram laid the grayish-pink strips of meat on to fry. The smell was almost a torture for Taylor. The cops had given them microwaved bowls of noodle soup, but her stomach was all empty again now. Apart from that, she was so glad to be home, and so deeply tired, she couldn't summon the strength to even remember everything else that had happened.

Gram smacked her hand when Taylor snagged a piece of bacon off the griddle and stuck it in her mouth, sucking air when it burned her tongue. It tasted wonderful.

By the time Mason came tumbling down the stairs, Taylor had eaten the first wonky undercooked pancake straight from the pan and filled a plate in the oven with the others.

Taylor heard Mason pound across the living room to the tree and rustle through the gifts underneath. Then he came galloping into the kitchen, stopping short when he saw Taylor. His pale round face was flat with shock.

Taylor wondered what Gram had told him. Did he think Taylor wasn't coming back? Her heart filled up, and when Mason all of a sudden hurled himself at her belly and threw his arms around her waist, she stroked his hair and hugged his shoulders, so small inside his child's skin.

Taylor's gift to Mason turned out to be a Playmobil Harvest Tractor set, which made her eyes go as wide as Mason's. She "gave" Gram a pair of driving gloves, and Douglas unexpectedly hugged her after he opened his box of chocolates. She got a painted macaroni necklace and a glittered card from Mason, and she immediately put the necklace around her neck and hugged him hard. Gram and Douglas gave her a new blue sweater that fit perfectly. She pulled it over her head, carefully avoiding her lip.

Finally Taylor heaved herself up and went into the kitchen to wash the dishes. She felt so tired, it was as if her bones had been hollowed out.

Lily had been sent to the hospital, and Taylor had wanted to stay with her, but the police made her go home with Gram. Now she wondered whether Lily and Devon were in the same place. What if they passed each other in the hallway?

The thought of Devon gave Taylor a sad lump at the base of her throat. He was no longer her boyfriend. It was ridiculous, but Taylor missed him. Or, not him, but the softness of the skin behind his ear, the clean-sweat smell of him after sex.

She thought of how Devon had destroyed her love for him. That was the worst thing he'd done. She wondered what would happen to him now.

She poured the bacon grease carefully into the coffee

can, watching the flecks of burnt meat slide through the thick yellow flow. It was hard to believe those brown bits and that slimy grease were once part of a living animal — a big grunting hog, but it was once a wee baby pig that loved the milk smell of its mother.

How did anyone get from nothing at all to a tiny bloom of cells (thanks, Mr. Assouad!) to a running, speaking boy clutching a Playmobil person in his fist — and then, eventually, back to cells? Then back to nothing again. Or, back to everything.

It was kind of comforting to think that being a person was, in a way, not normal. To make a person, your atoms separated themselves from the universe and turned into a thing apart. Then you wanted more than anything to stay apart, to be different and separate because you thought that was good for some reason. And you did everything you could to keep that apartness happening, feeding your body and protecting it from the weather and trying not to step in front of a speeding truck.

And then sooner or later when you died, you went back to normal, to being part of everything.

Taylor put the griddle in the sink and ran hot water over it. The water was burning her, but she left her hand under it for a moment, watching her skin get red, thinking about the urge she was having to pull her hand out to protect her physical self, separate from the universe. Then she did pull her hand out and squirted some pink dish liquid in and watched the bubbles foam up, tiny rainbows sliding across the round surface of each little ball of air.

Taylor scrubbed and rinsed the griddle, watching the last crumbs of once-pig wash away, put it to dry in the rack, cleaned the sink and dried her hands on the tea towel. It was a relief to be able to put something right. She drew a cigarette out of the pack Gram bought for her at the gas station on the way home.

She thought of Mason, of his body filled with blood and muscles and bones. His eyes that were like little pale galaxies if you looked straight into them.

Taylor ran up the stairs to Mason's room, where he was splayed on the floor with his new toys. She grabbed him and hugged him hard, laughing at his surprised expression. Then she sat cross-legged on the floor next to him and watched him play.

Twenty

IN THE END ALL THEY could do was send Lily home with painkillers. They had her change into a gown and she lay on a gurney in a hallway with an ice pack against her side and her rank clothes bundled between her feet. An orderly came by and guided the gurney out of its parking space and through hallways, into an elevator and then down more hallways. He parked her outside a yellow curtain, and she dozed until she felt herself being wheeled again. She posed for a series of X-rays, feeling like she'd been kidnapped by aliens who were studying her with their machines.

When the orderly returned, she summoned her courage and asked for something to eat. He stashed her in the hallway outside Emerg again and came back after a while with a couple of boxes of apple juice and a pair of puddings — one chocolate and one vanilla. Lily scarfed it all down. She swore to herself that as soon as she could she was going to get some real food. Macaroni with sauce. Or a cheeseburger. Whatever, followed by a wedge of chocolate cake. She would skim a ruffle of chocolate icing off the top and lick it off the edge of her fork.

Her mouth watered at the thought. Even the smell of sour vomit from a girl brought in with alcohol poisoning didn't stop her.

Eventually a young woman with long curlicues of hair rolling down her back came with a big Manila envelope, from which she pulled Lily's X-rays.

"Nothing's broken," she said briskly, holding the X-rays up as if to look at them, then immediately sliding them back into their sleeve. She gently lifted Lily's gown and then the ice pack, and winced at Lily's puffed, spectacularly bruised body.

"You probably have some bruising of the bones," she said, looking up into Lily's face for the first time. There was a pause. "Boyfriend?" she asked.

"Someone else's."

The doctor nodded. "That's bad," she said with a short laugh, which came out sounding surprisingly sympathetic.

The doctor wrote on her chart, then brought Lily some pills and a paper cup of water.

"You can go as soon as someone comes to pick you up," she said.

Lily looked down. She couldn't think what to do. Maybe her mother could find the money for a taxi?

"Is there someone at home to take care of you?" the doctor asked.

Lily considered. One could say too much in a situation like this.

Finally she raised her head.

"What kind of taking care do I need?"

The doctor cocked her head. "You should rest for a while, not do stuff. Not lift anything. So someone should bring you cups of tea and make your lunch and do your laundry. That kind." She watched Lily think. Then she went back to Lily's chart and read it again. "I can get social services to arrange something for you."

"No. My mom and I can manage." Lily thought of the twenty dollars still folded in her pocket. That would pay for a taxi. If she was lucky, her mom would be home and would either have smokes or enough money to run to the corner store for her.

The doctor looked at Lily for a moment.

"Why don't you have breakfast first," she said. Lily closed her eyes briefly, then lay back.

"Thanks," she whispered.

Lily ate from a tray balanced on her outstretched legs. The limp French toast, warm apple juice and watery coffee were ridiculously delicious.

She gathered her clothes and put them on in a bathroom, then walked as smoothly as she could to the exit. A nice taxi driver opened the door for her and looked sympathetic as she winced.

At home, Lily found her mom lying in bed, eyes open. She turned her head when Lily came in.

"You fucking bitch!" her mother shouted.

"You thought I was leaving you alone on Christmas?"

Her mother nodded, mouth turned down in an angry sulk.

"I'm here now," Lily said.

Her mother played with her sheet, twisting and untwisting it with her hands.

"I mad at you," she said, pouting.

Lily gripped the door. A wave of intense loneliness was making it hard to stand up.

"Sorry, Mom. I'm just late." She sagged against the wood. She knew that was a ridiculous thing to say after being AWOL for two days, but she also knew her mother would accept it. She wondered what it was like for kids with parents who actually kept track of them.

Lily gingerly shifted herself step by step toward the kitchen. Maybe she would stick that turkey in the oven anyway. In her coat pocket was the orange plastic container of painkillers the doctor had given her to tide her over until she could get to a pharmacy. Her warm feelings toward the doctor had disappeared when, holding the pills up but not handing them over, the woman had lectured Lily sternly not to share her meds.

In the kitchen, Lily leaned against the open fridge door and regarded the turkey in its cold plastic skin. It wasn't even the cooking that was such a problem. It was heaving the freaking thing up onto the counter, into the sink, into the roasting pan. And cleaning up would be a real killer.

She closed the fridge door and levered herself into a chair. Well, she could still make mashed potatoes, gravy and cranberry sauce. Her mother wouldn't care.

She opened the fridge again with her foot, and from her chair leaned in and took out the potatoes one by one, and the bag of cranberries and the margarine. Instead of filling the potato pot with water and then hauling it over to the stove, she put it on the stove and then filled it with cupfuls of water. She peeled the potatoes sitting down. She stood on a chair to take down the sugar for the cranberry sauce so she could lower it to the counter instead of raising her arms, which hurt too much.

She could hear her mother humming to herself in the living room. It made Lily glad to be home.

She poured the sugar onto the cranberries in the pot and turned it on, then sat heavily again. The kitchen began to fill with steam as the potatoes and the cranberries boiled.

She felt exhausted. Maybe they would just have their mashed with margarine. She couldn't face having to stand at the stove again to stir the gravy mix.

She heard her mother moving around.

"Mom," she called, but there was no answer. "Mom," she shouted, louder, although it pulled her side. She had never realized how many muscles it took to yell.

She was about to lift herself out of her chair when her mother came clattering through the door. Lily's eyebrows shot up. Her mother was smiling, and she had a length of gold tinsel garland thrown jauntily around her neck. She laid another garland around Lily. Then she held out a white cardboard box with a puffy bow on top, and looked at Lily expectantly.

Lily's vision blurred. She had not bought her mother a gift! She could feel tears lining up at the back of her throat, but she forbade them to come forward. Then she opened her eyes and pulled the bow off the box and stuck it on the side of her head.

"How does that look?" she asked.

"Good!" Her mom laughed happily.

Lily opened the box and stared at what was inside. She lifted it out. A medium-length cream wool scarf unfolded in sections.

The ache of knowing that her mother had somehow not noticed her multi-colored Most Impressive Scarf was eased by the fact that her mother had given her this unexpected gift.

Last Christmas her mother didn't even come home. Lily had no idea where she spent the day. Lily ate mac and cheese from the pot and then made a pan of brownies and decorated them with red sugar from the corner store. She stayed up late watching "It's a Wonderful Life" — a totally sappy movie — and eating half the pan of brownies with her fingers in a combination of self-indulgence and self-loathing. She'd bought her mother a portable alarm clock as a gift, hoping to encourage her in her attempts to keep a job. It sat in its wrapping on her mother's bedside table until sometime in February, when Lily noticed one day that it had been unwrapped. The time was never set.

Now Lily pushed herself up from the chair and shuffled into the living room. Her Most Impressive Scarf was hanging on one of the hooks next to the door. She saw that it was bedraggled, with stray fibers sticking out of the weave, a little stiff in places. She knew it must be a bit smelly. But she took it down anyway and brought it into the kitchen.

"Here, Mom," she said. "Would you like mine in return?"

Her mother took the scarf as if she'd never seen it before, and held it against her cheek.

"Sanks you, Lill-ll," she said, smiling.

And Lily smiled back as her mother wrapped the scarf over and over around her neck, burying the tinsel garland.

Twenty-one

TAYLOR PHONED LILY on Christmas night. Lily sounded thick and gravelly, although she brightened when she realized it was Taylor.

When Lily told her, laughing self-consciously, that they'd had mashed potatoes and cranberry sauce for Christmas dinner, Taylor packed up some leftover ham slices, a whack of candied yams that still had some marshmallows on top, and two slices of the fruitcake that Gram had been given at work. The next day she dropped Mason at Trevor's house, a plastic bag with his Playmobil pieces clutched in his fat mitten. Mason was actually panting as he galloped up the walk to Trevor's front door. It hurt Taylor's heart — in a good way — to see it.

Lily looked surprised and not particularly happy when she opened her door. Taylor held out the bag of food.

"I brought you some Christmas dinner."

Taylor could see Lily's face move through several

thoughts, but she wasn't sure what they were.

Then Lily smiled.

"Nice coat," she said, and Taylor smiled back shyly. Lily stepped back and held the door open. "My mom's out visiting one of her friends, but she could be back any moment."

"I can't stay that long," Taylor said. She kicked off her boots and followed Lily to the couch. She saw Lily walking stiffly, easing herself into a sitting position.

The ashtray was full and there were half-drunk scummy cups of cold tea and glasses of water on the side table.

"What did you bring?" Lily asked, pulling the foil-wrapped parcels out of the bag. She opened one of the bundles and delicately picked out a chunk of yam. She levered it up to her mouth with its marshmallow cap balanced on top, grinning sheepishly at Taylor as she chewed.

Taylor smiled. Lily swallowed and rewrapped the food.

"Thanks, T-Bone," she said quietly.

Taylor pulled out her cigarettes.

They lit up and sat in silence, smoking. Lily finished her cigarette and lay her head back against the couch. After a few minutes her eyelids closed and her lips parted slightly. Taylor watched the movement of Lily's eyeballs under the delicate twitchy skin of her lids.

It made her feel like a spy. So she got up and collected the cups and ashtray and went into the kitchen. She wiped down the stove, cleaned the sink, swept the floor and then, when she peeked and saw that Lily was still asleep, rummaged until she found a mop and bucket and mopped the floor. She was mostly done before it occurred to her that Lily might be offended by her cleaning up, but it was too late now.

She put the kettle on and made fresh cups of tea. A stink ran up her nose as soon as she squeezed open the milk carton. The spoiled stuff oozed out in thick clots when she tried to pour it down the sink. She ran the hot water until it steamed to chase the sour smell down the drain.

Sugar, then. She stirred an extra spoonful into Lily's tea and carried the cups out to the living room. She lit a cigarette for herself and one for Lily, then nudged Lily gently as she held the smoke out to her.

Lily opened her eyes, but she seemed to be surfacing from a far place. She looked lost. Taylor felt as if she was watching Lily through a one-way mirror. She wanted Lily to see her, but something was in the way.

"Lily," Taylor said gently. Lily slowly turned her head and the fog gradually evaporated from her eyes. Taylor smiled. She offered the cigarette, which gave off a thin gray thread of smoke that rose toward the ceiling, and the cup of tea, which steamed as if it could fill a tiny valley with cloud.

Lily extended a hand to take the cigarette, and then the other hand for the mug of tea, which she balanced on her thigh. Taylor took a drag off her smoke and sipped her own tea, silent and watchful. Lily was so stiff and slow, and she winced when she lifted her cup.

Taylor hadn't really thought before how Devon kicking the shit out of Lily was a way of saying, This is how little I care about you. Then that was true for her, too. When Devon punched her in the face. When he pinched her, slapped her, pulled her hair. When she said no and he pushed his way into her anyway. *You don't matter.*

When Bracken smashed Tannis in the face with the phone, when he blackened her eyes. When he killed her.

He was saying Tannis didn't mean a thing. And neither did Mason or Taylor.

So what did it mean when Tannis let Bracken treat them all that way? When Taylor let Devon abuse her?

Taylor dragged hard on her cigarette. She was aware of the tears streaming down her face, but she somehow couldn't connect them with anything. She was overwhelmed by the emptiness of her inside self.

She felt a shadow as Lily reached over to guide Taylor's hand past the arm of the couch to put her cup on the side table. Only then did she realize her hand had been shaking, and she had splattered some tea onto her leg. She felt Lily's cool hand slide briefly into hers, and then there was an empty space beside her.

She was sick with rage and shame, for herself and for Tannis.

Lily's hovering shadow returned, and Taylor felt her cigarette slipped out from between her fingers, a crumpled stiff wad of something pushed into her hand. She heard herself sobbing as Lily nudged her hand toward her face so she could wipe the snot from her upper lip.

A river was roaring through her, a wall of sound and the force of tons of whitewater pushing from the back of her head through her eyes and nose and mouth, coming out as water and snot and wailing.

Oh, Taylor thought. That terrible sound. What is making that terrible sound?

And finally, hearing the sound of her own sobbing and the feeling of all the wetness on her face, crawling down her neck and into her collar, brought her bursting back into the world. Next to Lily on the couch, Taylor collapsed against her and heard a soft whuff come up from Lily's chest, and Lily held Taylor and let her cry.

All the ravaging sadness that came through Taylor flooded out and was absorbed by Lily's T-shirt, then sank into the skin and bones of her shoulder and then further down into a deep well of goodness she kept inside her, where it disappeared, because Lily was so powerfully good.

"I'm sorry I hit you," Taylor sobbed.

"I'm sorry I hit you. I don't want to be that asshole." Lily chuckled softly, and it made Taylor laugh a bit, too, and then she cried even harder.

After a long time she quieted. She became aware of the mild, almost childlike smell of Lily's skin under the overlay of tobacco smoke. It was soothing, and she snuffed up as much snot as she could and then rooted her nose into the hollow of Lily's collarbone and let herself rest there and breathe it in.

It seemed like the first time in her life Taylor had been able to rest. She had never felt this before, ever. A narcotic heaviness invaded her, a dreamy loosening that detached her sinews from her bones. She heard the distant thump of Lily's blood traveling through her neck and behind her ear, and heard the passage of Lily's breath through her lungs and throat and out through her nose.

Lily's warm breath riffled a few strands of Taylor's hair, and it felt like a blessing of some kind. Lily was passing blessings through her hair with every breath, and tears began to seep through Taylor again, but this time they were not rivers of anguish but pearls of gratitude.

And if they hurt as they passed through her, she felt the wound was clean, perhaps even good.

Lily's hand eased itself over Taylor's back, as if the flesh had been laid open with a knife and she was smoothing it back into place, and Taylor felt the healing sink into her. She clutched the soft, worn fabric of Lily's T-shirt in one hand. Lily stroked Taylor's shoulder, her arm, and then slipped her hand between them and laid her open palm on Taylor's chest as if to hold Taylor's heart. And with Lily holding her heart like this, so she could be sure it would not burst out of her chest, Taylor let herself see in her mind's eye Tannis's body on the slab, her organs being packed in as if she were going on a trip, her corpse her suitcase. Her poor gray lump of a brain going in last through that violent hole in the chest.

And Taylor thought, maybe that's where it should end up, because what use is a brain if it is not where the heart is?

And then she burrowed closer into the warmth, bringing her own brain as close as she could to Lily's heart, and Lily hugged her gently back.

Author's Note

In the United States, almost 25 percent of adult women are beaten or raped by a partner. More than 15 million kids are exposed to abuse in the home every year. Girls and women aged 16 to 24 are most likely to be victims of violence from an intimate partner.[*]

In Canada, more than 40,000 arrests are made for incidents of domestic abuse and more than 400,000 sexual assaults are reported each year. Many incidents are not reported, so it certainly happens even more often than that.[†]

If you or someone you know has experienced abuse, *you are not alone, and it is not your fault.* No one deserves to be abused.

Below are the phone numbers and websites for some organizations that can help. In a crisis you can get immediate aid, or in a calmer time they can give you advice and point you to local resources. If you use a cellphone to call one of these numbers, or a computer to look at these websites, make sure no one who can hurt you can track your usage. A friend, a teacher or someone else you trust can help you find the strength to make the first contact.[‡]

Please take care of yourself, and be good to the people around you.

[*] National Network to End Domestic Violence (www.nnedv.org)

[†] Canadian Women's Foundation (www.canadianwomen.org/facts-about -violence)

[‡] Thanks to the Montreal Assault Prevention Centre (cpamapc.org) for help with this resource list.

UNITED STATES
National Domestic Violence Hotline/La Línea Nacional sobre Violencia Doméstica 1-800-799-SAFE (7233) or www.thehotline.org (English/español)
National Child Abuse Hotline 1-800-4-A-Child www.childhelp.org
State hotlines and coalitions www.feminist.org/911/crisis_state.html

CANADA
National Domestic Violence Hotline 1-800-363-9010
Kids Help Phone 1-800-668-6868
www.kidshelpphone.ca (English)
www.jeunessejecoute.ca (français)
National Child Abuse Hotline 1-800-4-A-Child www.childhelp.org
Tel-jeunes 1-800-263-2266 (English/français) www.teljeunes.com

For more information on the signs of abuse:
National Network to End Domestic Violence
www.nnedv.org/resources/stats/gethelp.html

Acknowledgments

First and foremost, warmest gratitude to my brilliant editor, Shelley Tanaka. This book has benefited enormously from her thoughtful, meticulous and highly skilled attention. I have, too — under Shelley's guidance I have learned as much again about writing as I knew before.

Thanks to Stephanie Lemieux — one of the smartest people I know and a wonderful friend — for giving me the scene that was the seed of this book, as well as timely and supremely useful input once the seed had started to sprout.

Sections of the book were written in bucolic retreats thanks to generous friends. One was written during a hurricane, with the loving companionship and protection of the much-missed Stormy. Thanks for that to unceasingly supportive friends Alisa Palmer and Ann-Marie MacDonald, with essential logistical support kindly provided by Alanna Palmer and Marven Palmer. Another was the result of a great week of separate work but shared hikes, meals and conversation with my dear friend Merrily Weisbord in the Laurentian Mountains.

My gratitude also goes to Sergeant Laurent Gingras of the Montreal Police Service for information about police procedures, and to Dr. Liam Durcan of McGill University and the Montreal Neurological Institute, who generously offered his medical expertise to a fellow writer. Any errors in the text are certainly my own.

I wish to acknowledge the financial support of the Conseil des arts et des lettres du Québec. A grant from CALQ allowed me to finish the first draft of this book. It was also a much-appreciated morale boost.

Last but most of all, thanks to Fred — for everything.

About the Author

Elise Moser was born in Brooklyn and grew up in small-town New Jersey. She went to McGill University in order to move to Montreal, and never left. She worked at Paragraphe Bookstore for twelve years and as a sales rep for American university presses with Lexa Publishers' Representatives for eighteen years.

Elise's short stories have been published in Canada and the US, and her adult novel, *Because I Have Loved and Hidden It*, was praised by the *National Post* as "[an] ambitious and artfully woven debut novel" when it was released in 2009.

Elise was president of the Quebec Writers' Federation between 2009 and 2012, and she works on issues of freedom of expression with PEN Canada and The Writers' Union of Canada. She presently divides her time between Montreal and Sauk City, Wisconsin.